T0196489

THE KING'S LAST RIDE

THE KING'S LAST RIDE

STEPHEN PATTERSON

iUniverse

THE KING'S LAST RIDE

iUniverse books may be ordered through booksellers or by contacting:

iUniverse
1663 Liberty Drive
Bloomington, IN 47403
www.iuniverse.com
1-800-Authors (1-800-288-4677)

ISBN: 978-1-5320-1707-0 (sc)
ISBN: 978-1-5320-1706-3 (e)

Library of Congress Control Number: 2017902061

Print information available on the last page.

iUniverse rev. date: 02/24/2017

Dedicated to those who have shaken their hips or worn blue suede shoes in memory of the King

Thank You - Thank You Very Much.

Special Thank You

I would like to thank the thousands of Elvis Presley fans who have not only kept his memory alive but have been instrumental in Elvis remaining one of the most influential performers of our time, long after his death.

CONTENTS

PREFACE

BIRTHDAYS AND ANNIVERSARIES ARE DATES most everyone can recall possibly due to the personal nature of the event. There are also dates in history that are remembered universally, dates that have had a great impact on society. There are events in life that take place that is so significant; the date becomes embedded in their memory. It's been well over fifty years since Donald Nuff a teacher at Jonesboro school entered our classroom and informed every one President Kennedy had been assassinated in Dallas Texas. The tragic date was November 22nd, 1963. I remember the date and the circumstances vividly. Six years later I also remember huddling around a Black n White TV to watch Neil Armstrong make his historic walk on the moon. It was July 20th, 1969, a proud day in American history. Much later in life as I was preparing for a business meeting when I was shocked to learn four planes were highjacked and turned into weapons of terror used against the citizens of the United States; it was September 11th, 2001. A horrifying day, for all America.

On such occasions, it's not unusual to remember where we were and what we were doing at the time, such events become headlines of our life. The dates we remember are the dates that impact us. Maybe it was how we felt about the event or how we viewed it the time.

Too many August 16, 1977, is such a date. On this date, many can recall where they were and what they were doing when they learned of the death of Elvis Presley. I was playing tennis with a friend when I heard the news. Why do I remember the date so well? Other rock n roll stars had died, and I don't remember the date or what I was doing when I learned of their death. But Elvis Presley was different he was more than a star he was a rock n roll icon. To many, he was the king of Rock n Roll as well as a movie and television star; Thousands loved Elvis. Many of his fans felt he was immune to the pitfalls of the normal man. How could Elvis die he was only 42, and he was one of the original cornerstones of rock n roll. How could he be gone? A question that was asked over and over as a nation prepared to say goodbye to the man and his career.

His death seemed to have impacted everyone from those who admired and loved him to those who just knew his persona as a rock n roll superstar. Elvis had been part of the music industry for over twenty-five years, and now his death was impacting society and the people who loved and admired him.

PROLOG

THE KING'S LAST RIDE

MARY FOUND IT EMBARRASSING HOW much she looked forward to reading and going through her mail. Maybe it was the journalist in her, but she preferred the hard copy over electronic. With email, you couldn't hold it or smell it leaving out anything remotely personal to the reader. Maybe it was her age that made her feel this way. That and the fact she was not proficient in social media.

Mary was in for the day the South Carolina weather was offering up the oppressive heat and the occasional afternoon thunderstorms. Today's mail was little different from other days'—an assortment of bills a few catalogs and grocery flyers, nothing personal unless you considered an invitation to a Pampered Chef Party personal. The only thing to strike her interest was a catalog from LL Bean nothing requiring her immediate attention. Mary had always been a sucker for a catalog. It was only mid-July, but the fall catalogs were now arriving. With the television supplying the background noise. Mary began to browse the catalog. Maybe she would discover the need for new hiking boots or stylish rain gear. For most of her adult life,

Mary had heard more television than she watched. A soundtrack of her life would include the noise generated by television. Seldom did she give the mindless chatter of the TV much attention? She had become a creature of habit, needing the sound more than for the entertainment. It was like flipping a light switch in a dark room a habit, not a necessity. If not for the sweltering heat, she may have missed the question.

Faith was once again playing a role in her life. Always a big believer in faith Mary had been fortunate through the year's others would say she was just lucky and faith had nothing to do with it. Mary preferred to believe faith guided her life. Feeling if she were indeed lucky she would have hit the lottery by now and those millions remained elusive. It made little difference whether you called it faith or luck, being in the right place at the right time shaped much of Mary's life.

Glancing through the catalog and with thunder roaring outside Mary heard the question. Bob Noe, the evening news anchor, asked the question pulling her attention away from the mail and to the television. Noe now had her full attention. Finishing up his six o'clock broadcast Noe asked, "How would you like to own the King's last ride?"

Noe liked to end his broadcast with a human-interest story; usually with little news value but entertaining. A tease to keep viewers tuned in. Tonight's tease grabbed Mary's attention—and with good reason. She was taken back in time to one of the most interesting and meaningful periods of her life.

Noe was reporting on a unique auto auction preparing to take place in Memphis, Tennessee. What made it interesting to Mary was the car set for auction, it just happened to be the hearse that carried the King to his grave, thus providing Elvis Presley his last ride. As soon as she heard the tease, she dropped her catalog and diverted her full attention to Noe and his report. The entertainment value did not stir Mary's interest or was she intrigued with the hearse value, and she certainly didn't have a desire to own the car. Her interest was personal. As Bob Noe was giving the details how one true Elvis fan could become the proud owner of the King's last ride, Mary began to recall the time she witnessed the last ride. Mary was fortunate enough to have been among the thousands of people who saw the hearse carry Elvis to his grave.

The events that surrounded that ride and the circumstances that brought her to Memphis some thirty years earlier had helped shape her life. Noe said a collector in Memphis, was set to honor the thirtieth anniversary of the death of Elvis Presley by auctioning off his prize possession the 1977 white Cadillac Eldorado hearse used for the funeral of Elvis Presley on August 18, 1977.

The collector saw the thirtieth anniversary of the death as a perfect time for the auction, fans from all over the world would be coming to Memphis to honor the King of rock 'n' roll. He recognized this was a big anniversary, and Mary felt it was also a perfect time to cash in on the Elvis phenomena. Every year the anniversary of Elvis's death thousands of fans would make the pilgrimage to Memphis. The thirtieth promised to be one of the biggest yet. Even in death, Elvis still had a loyal fan base, always ready and willing to honor his life. Noe reported, a representative from the auction house estimated the car could bring in as much as $200,000, a nice profit for the collector. With an aging fan base, the hearse may not hold as much value in the future. Though the King's followers remained strong, it was only natural to feel the numbers may begin to decline after all—thirty years can take a toll on any group. It was difficult for Mary to believe it had been thirty years three decades had passed since she witnessed the hysteria grip the city and nation once everyone learned of the death of Elvis Presley. An entire generation had grown up never having the opportunity to see or hear the entertainer live. Though Elvis had an immense catalog of music and films, Mary knew thirty years was an eternity in the entertainment industry even for Elvis.

Noe continued talking about someone having the opportunity to own a major piece of rock 'n' roll history. The anonymous collector would be using a local Memphis auction house; accepting bids over a two-week period with the high bidder announced on August 16, the actual anniversary of the death. The collector, a local Memphis businessman, purchased the hearse two years after the King's death, having bought the vehicle directly from the funeral home that handled the burial. The vehicle had been in the collector's possession for the past twenty-eight years. He was now referring to the hearse as the vehicle that gave Elvis, the King of rock 'n' roll, his last ride.

Noe gave more facts about the car and the collector after purchasing the hearse; the collector had kept the vehicle in a climate-controlled storage facility, protecting it from Mother Nature and time. For the two years, the collector didn't have possession of the hearse it had remained in the fleet of cars used by the funeral home up until his purchase. Sold at a public auction in 1979 the purchaser had received a document of authenticity certifying the hearse was the one that had transported the body of Elvis Presley from Graceland to Forrest Hills Cemetery on August 18, 1977. Noe told his audience the collector had amassed a large array of memorabilia from the funeral, as well as several other items from the career of Elvis Presley. The hearse was his largest purchase, and he had originally hoped to use it as an anchor to a museum dedicated to the life and career of Elvis. His dream of a museum died as Graceland became a public shrine to Elvis's memory. The collector saw little need to create another Elvis museum.

As Mary began to think of the sale, she wondered what one does with a used hearse. Her first thought was maybe an adventurous fan would purchase the car and begin making money selling commemorative rides through Memphis, the Graceland–Forest Hills–Graceland route. People certainly made money doing crazier things. Another thought was the owners of the Hard Rock Café should buy it and begin using it to offer patrons who had been over-served rides home. A limo service may want to retool the car and use it for special-occasion weddings or proms—the list was endless. Her thoughts then turned to decorating the hearse in Elvis paraphernalia—you could even get a life size Elvis sticker put on the side depicting the last ride. Whoever purchases the hearse would have plenty of opportunities to do what so many others have done in the past: make money from the memory and love of Elvis Presley. Mary felt certain whoever did purchase the car would probably put it into storage or a museum never actually using the vehicle, but she still enjoyed her fantasies of possibilities for the car. She knew whoever purchased the car would pay a high price when you consider what some have paid for collectibles over the past several years. Some crazy items had brought in thousands of dollars, from burnt toast resembling the Virgin Mary or macaroni favoring Jesus. There seemed to be a collector for everything and in many cases these collectors having more money than sense. The hearse would surely go either to an eccentric fan or a serious rock n roll collector. Indeed, there was a market for the car and surely would bring a sizable profit for the seller.

Noe and his co-anchor, Emily Shaw, were soon deep in mindless banter speculating on how much the hearse would bring. Emily's opinion most likely was influenced by her youth or lack of understanding for rock 'n' roll history. She wondered why anyone would be interested in the car. Emily was younger than the car itself and seemed rather naïve on the subject. In fairness to the young news anchor Shaw, she couldn't begin to imagine the symbolism the hearse represented in one of rock 'n' roll's more historical and memorial events. She saw it as a car, but to thousands of Elvis fans it symbolized the passing of a beloved entertainer; it was a vehicle used in marking the end of an era in rock music.

Even at her young age, Shaw was still older than Mary the day she witnessed the hearse give Elvis Aaron Presley his last ride. The hearse had a place in rock' n' roll history, but it also had a place in Mary's life. In 1977 there were no 24/7 news channels. It would still be another three years before Ted Turner introduced the world to CNN, signaling the birth of 'round-the-clock news. In today's news climate, every news outlet would have covered the funeral in every conceivable fashion to the point of ad nauseam. Even though in 77 the coverage was extensive, it would've been considered minimal by today's standards. In today's celebrity-crazed world, the funeral of a B-list entertainer demands more coverage than that given the King of rock 'n' roll in 1977.

Noe and Shaw continued their playful banter regarding the auction. Mary felt a few diehard Elvis fans would have considered the talk rather disrespectful, or even downright offensive. As the exchange continued, Mary began to drift back to a day in Memphis when she along with thousands of others, experienced the emotion, the turmoil, and the uncertainty of the last ride of Elvis.

Mary had not only witnessed the funeral, but she had experienced it, as well. Mary was lucky enough to have had a front-row seat to a dark chapter in rock 'n' roll history. Noe's simple question had brought it all back to the forefront of her memory.

In 1977 Mary would never have been considered a true Elvis fan though it was impossible to grow up and not be aware of his music and films. Even if she wasn't a fan, she was fortunate enough to find herself in Memphis for his funeral. Faith had shined on a small-town naïve reporter who received an assignment of a lifetime. That assignment unveiled an adventurous side of Mary, and it certainly was needed once she had the opportunity to cover the funeral. Not only was she able to cover the story but she would also live it.

The funeral attracted thousands as the attention of the world turned to Memphis Tennessee that hot August week. Drawing coverage usually reserved for a fallen world leader, not an entertainer. Many gave it the title: "Funeral of the Decade." Elvis may not have been a world leader, but make no mistake, he was a world figure. In the last thirty years, Mary had witnessed the funerals of presidents and heads of state, and the only funeral that even came close to the emotion and love found in Memphis back in 1977 was the funeral of Princess Di nearly twenty years later. Though many of his fans only knew him through his entertainment persona, it wouldn't keep the emotions and sorrow from being on display. For those in attendance, the occasion seemed more like a family funeral honoring a close relative not that of entertainer. There is a special relationship between entertainers and their fans, and Elvis was no exception.

Mary was drawn back to the newscast the weatherman Allan Cox was giving his two cents' worth. Cox told Emily not to underestimate the value and desire for such a vehicle; after all, they were talking about the King of rock 'n' roll. He rambled on about how the Rock-and-Roll Hall of Fame should enter the bidding or maybe the collector should just donate it to the Hall of Fame. His input prevented him from sharing the five-day forecast. Thirty years later; Elvis could still disrupt television.

Noe and his simple human interest story had stirred up Mary's memory. As the newscast came to an end, she began looking for an old photo album containing many of her memories of the Hearst, memories that had been stored away for years. Soon she located a cream-colored album sitting on a lower shelf, for Mary it was a time capsule of excitement. As she pulled the dust covered album from its perch, her memories began to flood her mind, as the loose clippings and faded photos fell from the album all helping to tell her story.

The aging album was a tribute to her brief time in Memphis that week back in August of 1977. The album represented a special chapter in her life. Though it had been years since she had looked through the collection, she had no trouble recounting the reasons she saved what she had. Taking the album over to the couch, Mary began her trip back in time, reliving her adventure. As she sat studying each item, a new sense of wonder came over her. Once again, her mind was awash with the memories of her short time in Memphis where she learned much about life while reporting on death. Everyone has significant moments in their lives. It could be the birth of a child or maybe the death of a close friend; there are many milestones in one's life, and this funeral was such a milestone for Mary.

That summer of 1977 Mary had graduated from college and turned twenty-two. At the time of Elvis's death, Mary had few life experiences; some would have said her world was ordinary and a tad boring. Of course, she didn't see it that way. She enjoyed college, from protesting the war to streaking down Main Street; she felt college always had something to offer and was far from boring. Though, when she accepted the job in Dublin Georgia, she had little knowledge of life away from Travels Rest, South Carolina, or Athens, Georgia. Most of her life had been in one or the other locale. Mary, like so many other college graduates, believed her diploma would open the world for opportunities, and there would be little else to learn. At twenty-two, she was ready to concur the world. It didn't take her long to realize there was always something to learn and she may not have been as ready as she originally thought. But many suffered from post-graduation illusions. One of the first lessons she learned was when it comes to dealing with people and human emotions; no one has a complete education.

Her collection from those few days in Memphis had limited real value, but she found it priceless. All, the photos, special items, and articles some she had written others she had collected soon gave her a path back in time, and she began to reflect on the funeral and the people she had met. Her mind was soon back in Memphis, and the circumstances that led her to learn so much about life while attending a funeral.

As a young reporter, Mary had difficulty understanding the emotional bond felt by fans when it came to their heroes. And Elvis was indeed a hero to many. Whether the emotions of the thousands of mourners gathered for the funeral were deserved or not, they left a lasting impression on Mary and how one's death can affect so many.

When Mary arrived in Memphis, she was not sure what to expect, but the reaction she witnessed was far different from what she had envisioned. So many fans considered Elvis larger than life. Far more than an entertainer to his true fans, he was something else—he was family, and he was the King. The emotional outpouring was difficult for Mary to understand. But now thirty years later she has an appreciation for it all, the people the emotions and the experience.

Mary's didn't feel the word funeral did the event justice. It was a funeral alright, but to the thousands who had come to Memphis, it was so much more. To some, it was a memorial celebration, and others referred to it as a grand farewell. Fan clubs from all over the world made the trip, hoping to send their hero off with a fitting tribute as they witnessed a beloved entertainer, laid to rest.

Mary knew Elvis through his music and public persona though many revered the man identifying him as a superstar to Mary he was just another entertainer. But all that changed once Mary came to Memphis where she witnessed the love of Elvis and how he impacted others' lives. The funeral gave her a personal lesson on life and love. She was unprepared for what transpired over those few days in Memphis she saw thousands upon thousands grieve dealing with the death of Elvis Presley. She had the rare opportunity to witness history first hand as a nation said goodbye.

Soon Mary found what she had been looking for, an aging newspaper article with the heading "Rock-n-Roll King Buried" by Mary McGill. It was her first exclusive and first page one report. The date was August 20, 1977. In the last thirty years, she had experienced her share of adventures. Her professional and personal lives had endured many ups and downs since those days as an assignment reporter for the *Dublin Journal* in Dublin, Georgia. Still, the adventure she found that week in 1977 remains a highlight of her life; she would have few adventures even come close to the experience. Mary was no longer, working in print journalism and there was no longer an evening paper in Dublin. But things were different thirty years ago; it was the evening paper of Dublin Georgia that Mary had hoped to launch her journalism career. The newspaper that gave her the opportunity to witness and report on the funeral. Relying on the kindness and support of strangers and the blessing of her Editor, Mary accepted the challenge and opportunity the funeral presented.

Elvis's death was a sad chapter in the entertainment world, but from his death, Mary received an education, not available in any schools. The assignment to cover the funeral gave her an up-close view of the many sides of humanity. Every emotion imaginable was on display: anger, sadness, joy, love they were all there. Mary also saw a city become a community as it celebrated and mourned the life of Elvis Presley.

Her assignment had given her a special view of life and death, a view few are privileged to see much less experience. Thirty years removed from it all the event still helps define her growth as a reporter and a person. The photos had begun to show their age, and the newspaper clippings were developing a yellowish tint from time and neglect. Looking through the memorabilia, reminded Mary of how fast time and life moves on. The entire event began to crystallize in her mind recalling how being in the right place at the right time had paid off; time could not remove the excitement she had felt.

Thousands wanted to be in Memphis when the news of Elvis's death broke, and thousands would come. Not only to pay their respects but also to be part of the memorial. One local Memphis restaurant owner felt the mourners resembled flies attracted to honey they couldn't get enough of it. For a few days in August of 77, the population of Memphis soared. Though thousands came, no one could have predicted what they would experience. No one truly knew what to expect especially Mary. Her assignment may have been simple; cover the funeral, but it was so much more. Mourners from every walk of life—rich, poor, black, white, educated, and uneducated—every socio-economic group had made their way to Memphis. Mary became overwhelmed by the number of people who traveled to Memphis, making her want to know more about why. She was seeking answers to questions she didn't know how to ask. Why had people come? What were they hoping to find?

The questions everyone asked was how could he be dead and why did he die. The questions were more of a rhetorical nature as so many wrestled with the news of the death. Unfortunately, few would find the answers they sought. Mary learned in journalism school questions based on emotions rather than rational thinking; the answer is seldom satisfying. Many felt the timing was unfair. But then again, is any death fair? A great number of his fans felt abandoned—they had lost a hero in the prime of his life. Talent doesn't guarantee a longer life. Mary believed even though the questions exsisted, few were willing to accept the answer.

The funeral only added more questions. Thirty years later several questions remained that was the power of Elvis. Over the years, there has been plenty of speculation and a fair number of fans holding on to the belief that Elvis was still alive, all supported by rumored sighting none of which verified, but all adding to the legend of Elvis and giving his fans false hope. When it comes to the death of Elvis, the truth may never be known or at least never accepted.

A fan who came from Illinois told Mary she wanted a story to tell her grandchildren. Everyone would leave Memphis with an impression and a story. From the hardcore to the casual fan, all would be affected. In three short days, what started out as a funeral to say goodbye to an entertainment icon became much more. It became a statement of how humanity dealt with death and lost.

Though considered a member of the press, Mary knew she fell somewhere between a curiosity seeker and a reporter. She had limited experience and never reported on anything remotely as huge as the funeral. Her journalism credentials were far from impressive, so even she considered herself an observer.

When Mary arrived in Memphis, she had several professional goals. She hoped to gain a perspective on the funeral and share it with the readers in Dublin. Originally, she was little different from other reporters looking for any angle that would stimulate readers and discussion. Mary wanted to give the reader in Dublin a feel for being in Memphis. It was a noble goal but may have been a result of an overactive ego. She discovered a story unfolding in Memphis that would take more than her journalistic capabilities. As a journalist, she wanted to give the readers a taste of the action. But the sheer magnitude of the event made that almost impossible. There was a story to tell, and Mary was there to do it. Her thinking may have been a little grandiose, but her twenty-two-year-old confidence made her feel she could handle it all.

Every hour Mary spent in Memphis the magnitude of her story grew. She became entangled in a side show of emotions. The grief on displayed overwhelmed men women and children some couldn't keep their tears in check. There were those who questioned the media and even some who questioned the government. No one wanted to believe Elvis was gone and the people she encountered in Memphis gave her memories she would cherish for years to come.

When it came time for Mary to put words to paper, her biggest challenge was separating the real story from all the accompanying chaos. She often compared the experience to attending a circus with the funeral being the center attraction, but unlike a true circus, three rings could not do the funeral justice. It was something to see, and for this circus, no ticket was necessary. Every death has a story, but when the deceased is a celebrity, you can expect the stories magnified.

Though Elvis had been entertaining for longer than Mary had been alive, he was still considered young. His career had provided so much pleasure to his adoring fans that she knew before reaching Memphis his funeral would stir emotions and controversy. The legacy of Elvis Aaron Presley would continue to grow. His recording and acting career had a profound impact on the world, and his funeral was just more of the same. His unexpected death left a void for millions of adoring and heartbroken fans. A heartbreak felt throughout the world.

Mary smiled coming across a photo of some of the friends she made in Memphis there was plenty of excitement and adventure, but the biggest bonus for Mary were the friendships she made. No matter what brought you to Memphis when you left, you were different. Everyone in attendance would be affected it was that powerful. The emotions were only part of the story. There was also intrigue, tragedy, and suspicion. As fans gathered to say goodbye to a rock 'n' roll icon, people began to realize how much they shared with others from around the globe. They may have been strangers in the beginning, but their love of Elvis bonded them together.

With a loud clap of thunder and the flickering of the lights, Mary was soon alone with her thoughts. Her house was now quiet and with the quiet came reflections on her few days in Memphis.

SHE GOT THE JOB

Mary had just finished sitting through the weekly meeting of Dublin's Uptown Rotary and a presentation from Raymond Tucker of Georgia Power. Tucker talked about the growth of nuclear power and safety ramifications for the future. Covering the Rotary was a regular gig for Mary. Meeting every Tuesday, for lunch at the Fairview Dairy Bar whose tag line proclaimed, "It's fresh from Moo to You." Tucker went a little longer than usual, but she was finally in her car and on her way back to the office. The C&S Bank sign offered up information Mary didn't want. But there it was flashing the time, 2:20 p.m., and then the temperature a large green ninety-eight appearing. No one needed a flashing green sign to know it was hot. Dublin had hot summers, but ninety-eight was an exception, not a rule and there was no one needing an endorsement from the C&S Bank. Considering the temperature and the humidity everyone was guaranteed a rather miserable afternoon it was hot and sticky.

With a full-time job Mary now felt the heat more than in the past. Her friends who had yet ventured into the world of permanent employment would say she had an RJ or a real job. The RJ gave her a new set of responsibilities and concerns. While in school, she had few cares, and one of the lesser ones would have been the weather. Grudgingly, she had accepted the fact that life was different. A summer of change she was now focusing on needs rather than wants. Starting this new chapter in her life, she decided to focus on the positives and welcome the challenges while addressing the responsibilities.

On the day, Mary graduated from the University of Georgia, her father gave her a hug and proclaimed she would be embarking on a new path in life. College was behind her, and the work world lay ahead. Her dad had said;

"Pumpkin the next few months will set the stage for the rest of your life. You will be transitioning from full-time student to full-time employee. And you will find that the work world is very different."

His pet name for her was "Pumpkin." As a child, she had considered it cute, but the older she got, the less flattering she found it and was not at all excited about his declaration concerning work.

The jobs she held while in schools never required her to work forty hours a week. She had spent most of her college summers behind a cosmetic counter at Belk's in the Colonial Mall back in Greenville, South Carolina. With a flexible schedule, she could always find time away from the counter to enjoy her summer. Now, totally removed from the spray perfume and lip gloss the office had replaced her days at the cosmetic counter. With an office came real duties and fewer avenues of escape. But it also came with an upside: she had a salary-paying job. Something many in 1977 couldn't say. Her parents would say she was for once making money rather than just spending it. But with the additional money came additional bills. As she began to turn into the parking lot of the Dublin Journal, she proclaimed aloud, "You're not in Kansas anymore," a favorite saying of hers since starting this chapter in her life.

Mary found refuge from the afternoon heat in her office at the

Journal. Serving as her personal oasis the converted broom closet was her home away from home. So small her roommate Sherry told everyone Mary would have to go outside it to change her mind. But to Mary, the converted closet gave her a feel of acceptance she was a journalist working for an honest to goodness newspaper beating the cosmetic counter any day. It was a makeshift office, smelling of a combination of Johnson Wax and Pledge. The centerpiece was a gray steel desk that showed the wear and tear of years of use. Mary often daydreamed of the stories the desk could tell. The desk accented by an aging blue upholstered chair and an old four-drawer tan filing cabinet, leaving little room for anything else. On the desk sat her Royal electric typewriter. Folders scattered over the desk—paid homage to her efforts as a reporter. She had tried to brighten the office with photos of home and the University of Georgia. On the back, wall hung a print of Sanford Stadium, home of the Georgia Bulldogs. A small bulletin board hung on one wall covered with postcards and well wishes from friends and family.

The assortment of postcards came with a downside considering many of the cards were from friends who had not entered the work world and were traveling discovering themselves. At times, Mary felt a little envious of these friends who had delayed their jump into full-time employment. Occupying a corner was a testament to her lack of horticultural skills. It was a small green flowerpot with a dying flower. Who knew that plants required water and sunshine regularly? The flower had been a gift from her mother. The gift surprised Mary knowing her Mother was keenly aware of her luck with plants. Mary jokingly told her mother she hoped her tenure with the paper would last longer than the plant, and now it was safe to say she had reached this goal. It was clear from the dying leaves and dried soil; she once again was on the verge of losing another battle with Mother Nature.

Fortunately, her writing skills were greater than her farming skills. The once beautiful plant that blossomed with such promise was well on its way to becoming a dying memory.

She could find joy in her workspace no matter its drawbacks. In this little space, Mary could focus on her assignments and reflect on her writing as it gave her a place to call her own. She found the nameplate that adorned the front of her desk to be proof positive that she was putting her degree from the University of Georgia to use. She felt fortunate to be working at all with the economy in a downturn; everyone was being affected especially recent college graduates. Mary was appreciative to the staff and management of the *Journal* and the opportunity given her—to work in her chosen field of study and pursue her dream. After accepting the job Mary told her parents, she hoped the *Journal* would be the first rung on her personal ladder of success.

The Journal had a decent circulation—a little over twelve thousand regular subscribers and even more readers—for a community the size of Dublin, it was considered a success. The paper was published six days a week, Monday through Saturday. The larger cities covered Sundays. It was locally owned, though the owners seldom made an appearance. The paper's mission was to serve the citizens of Johnson and Laurens counties with the current nonbiased news. A plaque in the receiving lobby read, "News you can trust, Opinions you can consider, offered by people you know." In many ways, the words rang true, as the editors sought neutrality rather than adversity.

Irish immigrants originally settled the area and town of Dublin, and they chose the name Dublin honoring their Irish heritage. The hilly terrain also resembled that of the capital of Ireland. Dublin though a small town did offer some diversity many associated with a larger community. Mary was pleasantly surprised at how much she liked the paper and the citizens of Dublin. She found both to be just what the doctor ordered. Though she was relatively new to the area and still learning the ends and outs of the job, she felt she had made the right decision and had chosen the proper career path.

The *Journal* was little different from other small-town papers. The wire service tear-offs covered the national stories. Firsthand reporting dealt with local stories and events. There were times that the national news would spill over into the local news and vice versa. Especially true when it came to President Carter and his home of Plains Georgia, less than a hundred miles from Dublin you could count on some stories coming out of Plains. Billy Carter, the president's infamous younger brother, often made an appearance in Dublin. The editor of the paper believed that putting a local slant on the national news helped give the paper a much larger feel.

Billy Carter and his antics supplied plenty of opportunities for stories. Years before President Carter was elected, his brother, Billy, had taken over the day-to-day operation of the family peanut business. Sadly, many in the town and probably the country considered Billy Carter to be little more than comic relief when it came to covering the Carter family, and with his redneck, good-ole-boy persona, he presented quite a contrast to the thirty-ninth president of the United States. As the saying goes, you can pick your friends, but you can't pick your family. Billy seemed to present a challenge to the Carter White House, and Billy was battling the notoriety of being known as the "First Brother" of the United States. One venture of Billy's was to capitalize on his fame and love for beer, and in the spring of 77, he introduced to the world "*Billy Beer*." After lending his name and image to "*Billy Beer*," he became the spokesperson for the product, and this brought him to Dublin often. Soon after Mary arrived in Dublin, Billy Carter came to town hawking his not-so-tasty delight.

He was set-up at a local convenient store, and people could have a photo made with him or get his autograph and, of course, buy some of his product. It was quite an event. Billy appeared to be a willing participant when it came to capitalizing on his brother's fame.

It was at this event that Mary received her first assignment she was asked to cover Billy Carter giving the readers a little insight into the life of someone so close to the most powerful man in the world. Mary found Carter had an engaging personality and was easy to talk to; it was hard not to like him. Though she was sure hundreds of different reporters had asked him the same questions, he took the time to answer all her questions and did so in a fashion that made her feel as if it was the first time he had heard them. That is what she liked best about him. Mary concluded after their meeting that family dynamics could be challenging no matter where life takes you.

Most of the readers enjoyed both the *Journal* and the *Atlanta Constitution.* The *Constitution* was a morning paper covering state and national affairs. The *Journal* came out in the afternoon and covered local stories. Reporting on the town gossip was also a part of the *Journals* coverage. Gossip and local tidbits featured in such columns as *Rambling in Dublin* and the ever popular *What's Up on Main.* A resident of Dublin was encouraged to share any information they may have regarding personal or family news. Like most small-town papers, a mainstay of the operation consisted of local weddings, graduations, deaths and local sports. This summer the success of the local American Legion team was also a hot topic. Like most southern cities football was king and with the High School's starting to practice especially the team from Dublin High the Fighting Irish would garner a lot of print. If you read the *Journal,* you had no excuse not to know what was going on in and around the town.

Neither, the paper or the town of Dublin were in Mary's sight following graduation. But faith sometimes takes you down a different road. No one could have imagined her ending up in a place like Dublin or working for a paper such as the *Journal.* Her only knowledge of Dublin was the legendary famous St. Patrick's Day festival they held every year. No surprise that a town named for the Irish capital would have a rowdy St. Patrick's Day party. The celebration was sheer fun, drawing thousands to eat, drink, and party. Dublin's population could double on St. Patrick's Day; drawing partiers from all over the state.

Even though Mary attended the University of Georgia, she never figured she would end up in Georgia. Raised in the foothills of South Carolina, not far from the Georgia line, she just felt she would return home and make her start there. Like so many coming out of college, she had more questions than answers when it came to her future. Though it was not the career path she had envisioned, it was the path she had chosen. So today, she was making a living and enjoying life in the town of Dublin Georgia.

In school, Mary had dreamed of working for one of the big pretentious newspapers. She often fantasized about being recruited by one of the big boys like the *Washington Post* or *New York Times* or even the *Miami Herald*; she wanted to do great things for a great paper. Her dreams might have said more about where she hoped to live rather than where she wanted to work. Mary desired a career in investigative journalism, writing stories that would earn her a front-page byline and impact the community and the world. She may have been a little grandiose with her dreams, but that is why there called dreams. She was a big dreamer. Her parents had always told her to dream big, and Mary had no problem following their advice. One of her father's favorite expressions was "If you can't go, first class, why to go at all?" Of course, she'd never been a first-class traveler nor had her father for that matter—he was from a rural community in North

Carolina and had been raised during the Depression, so his idea of first class and hers might have been somewhat different. She knew the world could always use a good reporter and if so why not her?

Mary soon realized that there was a big divide between her fantasy world and reality. She recorded it in her journal as "'Reality,' and 'Fantasy' seldom share the same headline." She received a strong education about life with her assignments and local stories. As a famed philosopher once said, "Every journey begins with a single step," and her journalism career was beginning with, tiny steps in Dublin, Georgia. The Pulitzer would have to wait unless someone thought a feature on Jan Union's chicken salad at the annual July 4th picnic merited one.

She developed an appetite for major stories while reporting on President Nixon and the RNC ill-fated Watergate break-in that occurred during her freshman year in college. The work she did on the break-in was limited to recounting the hearings and reporting on the action. But her appetite for an investigation grew while watching Sam Irvin lead the hearing. It was a sweet assignment for a reporter with dreams of greatness. The entire nation was following the scandal, a scandal of such magnitude it led to impeachment hearings for the president and eventually his resignation from office. Stories don't get much bigger than that, at least not in Athens, Georgia.

College campuses across the United States were also dealing with student unrest growing out of an unpopular war in Vietnam and the general mistrust of the government. Mary saw it as a good time to be in college. Those turbulent years of political unrest made for good theater and gave her plenty to write. The downside of starting out with such a big story was as a naïve college freshman; she believed she was destined to write great stories of interest and importance. Unfortunately, in Dublin, there were few assignments that called for investigative skills, and if she hoped to become the female equivalent of Bob Woodward, those dreams were now on hold.

Even though it wasn't the *Washington Post* or the *Atlanta Constitution*, she was surprisingly happy with her choice. When considering the job offer, Mary wondered if she would be happy. Her parents were just excited and relieved to know she had a job. Though they would never admit it, both were a little worried about their investment in her education, wondering if it would result in real work. Mary was hesitant about accepting the position in Dublin and shared her feeling with her mother; it was her mother that asked a valuable question: "At twenty-two, who knows what they want?" Her mother felt she should be thankful for the opportunity and make the best of it. Not a strong endorsement for the job, but it did make sense. Mary's mom was optimistic telling her that if she worked hard and made smart decisions good things would follow. The other papers never made an offer or even gave her an interview making the decision to come to Dublin that much easier.

Mary's journey to Dublin was not conventional she had sent out her fair share of resumes and applications with little success. It was her college advisor Dr. George Troxler who suggested she look for a position with a small-town paper. Dr. Troxler believed that a smaller paper would be the best place to start, she could get the experience she needed for other opportunities later in her career. He felt the best reporters learn from the bottom up; such experiences gave the reporter the ability to identify and communicate more successfully with the reader. Troxler made his case telling her a smaller paper would allow her to learn and develop a style all while sharpening her reporting skills. Troxler liked to use the analogy that journalism was like baking a cake. If you were going to have a winning recipe, you needed all the ingredients. The ingredients would have come together with knowledge and skill before the cake went in the oven. The school would provide some of the ingredients, experience the rest both leading to real success. He believed the root to career satisfaction came when experience and knowledge merged with personal desire. "Your education makes the experience more meaningful, and when you find meaning in your life, you will then find satisfaction," he said. And to Dr. Troxler, the ingredients in the newspaper business meant learning every aspect of it from delivery to sales the more you experienced, the more you understood.

While conducting her shotgun approach of resumes and applications Troxler learned of an opening with the *Dublin Journal*, and without her knowledge, recommended they consider Mary for a position. Even before Mary knew about the job, the paper's editor, Charles Alexander, had received a recommendation from Troxler that he consider Mary. Alexander had been a student of Troxler's while attending the University of North Carolina during the '60s. When Troxler suggested Mary, the timing was right she was having no success with her search. With no real prospects in sight, Mary jumped at the opportunity to interview, and the rest is history. Two old friends had reconnected, and she was the beneficiary. Soon after the interview, she made a move to Dublin where she was learning the newspaper business in a fashion that would make Troxler proud, from the ground up. The job and duties were different from those she had while working for the student paper the *Red and Black*. But the biggest difference was she was getting paid. Though it wasn't much, it was still the most she had ever made.

Starting out in Dublin only solidified her knowledge that the bottom of the ladder of success is still the bottom. Though her business cards proclaimed assignment editor, she still did her fair share of running for other reporters. Mary began to work the same week she moved to Dublin, realizing the sooner she started the better she would be financially and emotionally, leaving little time to be homesick.

She had little concern over the assignments that came her way just so long as they kept coming. She was enjoying the work and learning plenty she felt welcomed and needed; she had made a good choice. She found her challenges where she could. If she was reporting on potato salad, then you could bet the assignment was going to get her utmost attention and best effort.

Most of her early assignments offered few challenges but she was gaining experience, and as Dr. Troxler had emphasized, the experience was the fuel for success. It had been years since the paper had hired a new reporter, and her hiring was a positive sign for everyone an indication the paper was growing. The veteran reporters were glad to have her on board.

Mary sat her ego aside and began cutting her journalistic teeth on flower shows and senior citizen banquets. She had already covered a Billy Carter lookalike contest at a local nightspot, and last week, she had done a feature on the first harvest of the Dublin Garden Society's *Garden of Hope*, which was planted and grew vegetables for local seniors unable to maintain their personal gardens. In eight short weeks, she had become part of the community. Mary was beginning to feel at home in Dublin, and the people and stories meant something to her.

Her first permanent assignment was not very uplifting, but it was regular work. She was assigned to cover the obituaries desk. Even in Dublin, the obituaries needed attention, and unfortunately, there was a steady number of citizens in need of the service. Before arriving at the paper, the obits rotated among the other reporters. The upside for her everyone had some experience in writing obits, and if she needed assistance, she didn't have to look far.

Waiting on her desk was her latest assignment a short handwritten note from Nancy Cannon, a senior reporter. Nancy had taken a call from Rogers Funeral Home reporting the death of an elderly gentleman named Lance (Lanny) Bryson Cole.

Mary placed a call to Bill Miller with Rogers Funeral Home after reading Cannon's note. She would need some information for the obituary, and the funeral home usually supplied it. The funeral home would collect information from family members and share it with the paper along with any special request for the write-up. Usually, a loved one would fill out a questionnaire designed to help gather information that would be helpful in the obituary. Mary had mixed feeling regarding the questionnaire though she had never been present when someone was asked to complete the questionnaire. Mary felt it may be a little burdensome for a grieving family; she hoped it would serve as a mechanism to remember the positives of the loved one and not open any old wounds. But she also knew the questionnaire was helpful, giving her the families input. Mary's goal was to write an obituary that would make the family proud. At time obituaries, can be impersonal and difficult. The collected information allowed Mary to learn more about the deceased and enabled her to add a personal touch to the completed obituary.

Not all the information ended up in the final write-up, but in the newspaper business too much is better than too little. Miller told her the packet had been dropped off and they were hoping to have the announcement in the next day's paper. A deadline for the dead made Mary smile.

She located the packet at the receiving desk and returned to her office and began reading the information. Mr. Lance Bryson (Lanny)

Cole was a native of Lauren County had died the night before after a lengthy battle with lung cancer. The obit was restricted to a three-inch column but could be increased for a modest fee if the family desired there was also a charge for a photo to accompany the write-up. The funeral home paid for the article, and they would pass the charge on to the family members. In the short time, she had been writing the obits few families requested increased space. Photos did generate a fair amount of revenue. Attached to the questionnaire was a photo of a much younger Cole.

> *Mr. Lance Bryson Cole 85 died peaceably at his home following an extended illness on August 15th. Mr. Cole was a graduate of Trenton Normal School for Boys in Trenton Georgia. Known to friends and loved ones as Lonnie he had been a lifelong resident of Lauren County. A charter member of the Dublin Kiwanis Club Mr. Cole was known for his charity and compassion toward others. Preceded in death by his loving wife Ethel Howard Cole a son Sgt. Martin S. Cole who died while serving in the Pacific during World War II. Mr. Cole was considered a true gentleman who touched the lives of everyone he knew. A decorated veteran having served in the United States Army Air Corp. during the first World War receiving the Purple Heart and other medals of valor for his participation in the European conflict. He is survived by sons Lonnie Bryson Cole Jr. and his wife Dorothy of Evansville Ga., William R. Cole of Dublin and a daughter Kathy Cole Biggs and her husband Donald of Atlanta Ga. as well as numerous grandchildren and great-grandchildren. Services*

Mary was putting the finishing touches on Mr. Cole's obituary; when she was startled by a phone call. She hardly had time to give her name when she realized it was the managing editor Charles Alexander. A rare treat for Mary normally if Alexander wanted her he would just summons her with his loud authoritarian voice. The distances between the two offices did not offer a challenge when it came to seeking someone out.

With his voice, he could get your attention in a hurry. It was rare enough to get a phone call, but one from Charles was especially rare. Since coming to the paper, most of her assignments came from Lewis Stewart, the assignment editor. But Lewis was out, so today she was getting attention from the top. Her newness to the job made her a bit intimidated by a call from Alexander.

Her anxiety only intensified when Alexander confirmed he had an assignment for her. She was excited at the thought that Alexander would be given her an assignment. Mary didn't want to appear too eager, so she questioned him if she needed to follow up on the adventures of Ms. Fulton's cat or investigate another one of her UFO sightings.

One of her first assignment at the paper was to interview Debra Fulton, an elderly lady who regularly called the paper. Ms. Fulton no one dared call her Debra was a lifelong resident of Dublin and had lived in the same house on Lee Avenue for over 80 years. She had developed quite a reputation for her reports. Most of the staff felt she viewed the paper as an extension of her family and like a loving sister she never hesitated to call. Ms. Fulton's ability to get around was getting harder for her, and her eyesight had begun to fail, and both contributed to her calls. She tended to see things that weren't there or to misinterpret what she did see. Leading to regular calls about UFO sightings especially after learning President Carter had once claimed to have seen one. Another favorite topic for Ms. Fulton was her pet cat, Murphy. Murphy was an overweight tabby that unfortunately had no trouble climbing trees the trouble came in getting down. The adage what goes up must come down didn't always apply to Murphy. Mary was asked to interview Ms. Fulton when she celebrated her 85th birthday. Mary discovered she was a delightful lady and was loved by everyone. She was often mentioned in the Rambler section of the paper when the family would visit. Rambling in Dublin was a short column found on the left side of the front page. It was a nice way to personalize the happenings of Dublin. Some referred to the Rambling section as a printed party line everyone could learn a little something by reading *Rambling in Dublin.*

There was an air of excitement in Charles's voice when he told her she might find the assignment interesting and would probably thank him later, only increasing her nervousness. Mary took a deep breath and told him she was hooked and ready. "What's the assignment?"

Mary knew Charles was a respected professional. If he felt it was a good assignment then it must be, the newspaper business was in his blood he loved the process of getting the story, formalizing it and sharing it with the readers. He lived by the credo (find the news write the news and share the news). He also believed you should always be looking for the next story. He was not one to waste time or effort. When Mary interviewed for the job, he shared his philosophy of the newspaper business, telling her the paper's product was the news. And in reporting the news, you needed to be professional and demonstrate care, emphasizing with every story someone would be affected.

Charles began telling Mary that the associated press had just announced that per a hospital spokesman in Memphis Tennessee Elvis Presley had died. The official announcement made around 3:30 PM and the news was creating quite a firestorm across America and the world. Though Charles continued to talk, she heard very little after hearing Elvis was dead. She was shocked and finally asked Charles for clarification. She stopped him in mid-sentence. "Did you say Elvis Presley is dead?"

Charles paused for a moment giving her an opportunity to collect her thoughts. He then said, "That's the report." Charles in a rather non-reverent tone added;

"Mary, it seems that old swivel hips next performance is in that great honky-tonk in the sky."

Before she could comment on his lack of taste in describing the death, Charles became serious. He told her the story would obviously, have an impact on a lot of people, and he felt everyone would be talking about the death and when people are talking the paper needs to be reporting. Charles felt the national coverage would be extensive leaving the responsibility of the *Journal* to cover the news of the death locally. He continued;

"Mary I realize I'm stating the obvious, but this is a huge story. The news of Elvis's death will grip Dublin the nation, and the world. People will be emotional, and the Journal needs to handle it with the utmost respect. Even though the story will be broadcasted and rebroadcasted and every news outlet will tell it. I want to be proactive on how we cover it. To be proactive, we will need an angle for our coverage. And I feel that angle is how the citizens of Dublin remember Elvis and how his career affected them".

Alexander questioned Mary why she thought people read the *Journa*l. She realized this was a rhetorical question and before she could say anything he gave her his answer.

"The citizens of Dublin read the *Journal* because they want a local feel to the news they want to know what is happening down the block and up the street. And the death of Elvis is going to stir a great deal of talk throughout town. We need to give the readers that local perspective. Elvis was far more than an entertainer; the news of his death will create an emotional story a story that needs our attention."

Charles told Mary to concentrate on the emotional side of the news, get people's reactions. The angle Charles wanted the paper to take was to look at how people were reacting to the death, not the death itself. She should learn how the citizens of Dublin were being affected by the news. He asked her to speak to the traditional and nontraditional fan get a feel for how everyone is handling the news. Charles felt it would be a topic of conversation in the beauty parlors, the drug stores, and the supermarket's, people are going to have an opinion, and where there is an opinion, there is a story. Telling her;

"This kind of news stirs up all kinds of reactions. Years from now people will be able to tell you where they were and what they were doing when they heard of the death of Elvis."

In addition to the emotional story, Charles hoped to uncover the human side of how Elvis and his music impacted the lives of those in Dublin. Knowing as a rock n roll legend, Elvis had touched many with his music, and there would be stories to share from those who loved him. Charles reminded Mary Elvis had been a superstar for a long time noting everyone should have something to share.

Mary began to think how fortunate she was getting this assignment; maybe there was something to being the last reporter in the building. She wasn't naïve enough to think that this would have been her assignment if others were still at the office.

Charles instructed her to drop what she was doing (after all Mr. Lance Bryson Cole would still be dead when she returned) he wanted her to go to the hospital and do some interviews. He suggested she talk to a variety of people. Mary knew she would have little trouble getting a sample of the public's reaction. The news would be spreading, and almost everyone would be processing it. He asked her to concentrate on the story within the story. He added people would be looking for support asking questions hoping to find answers to that age-old question *why*? Mary felt the death would continue to make headlines for days to come. She believed she needed to proceed with caution and be as respectful as possible in her interviews.

Mary agreed with Charles on how to approach the story, and she knew the hospital was a good place to start. One of the first lessons she received from Charles was if you want the public's reaction to an event you needed to go to the most public place possible and to Charles that was the hospital.

Charles said he would give Gary Jackson the hospital administrator a call to clear her way with the interviews. Telling her he was certain Gary would approve after all Gary always liked seeing the hospital's name in print, publicity is publicity.

After hanging up the phone, Mary gathers a few items and on her way out stopped by Charles's office to quickly review the wire reports. The more knowledge she had, the better equipped she would be for the assignment. Though excited, she was also a bit anxious knowing if she did a good job on this assignment more such assignments could come her way. Entering Charles's office, it was clear he was talking with Gary Jackson. Mary smiled as she heard Charles deliver his pitch for her to come to the hospital. The call was little more than professional courtesy. Gary was on board with the interviews allowing him to give Mary the thumbs up. After some idle chatter about playing golf, the call ended. Mary was now the lead reporter on a major story.

Charles told Mary to check the teletype before leaving saying it had been humming since the story broke and then handed her some of the copy already pulled. This death of Elvis Presley was generating attention throughout the world. Mary felt somewhat guilty about her excitement for the assignment knowing how others were reacting to Elvis's death.

Mary began to contemplate the magnitude of the news. The reports she read presented a pattern of information. The lead, was the death, coming in a close second was the reaction to the news what people were saying from dignitaries to fans, the least reported item dealt with the circumstances of the death. As Mary glanced over the reports, Charles began to give his take on the news.

He felt the news would be difficult for some to accept especially those hardcore Elvis fans. Before leaving Charles's office, Mary thanked him for the assignment and the opportunity. It was nice to think he believed in her abilities and she assured him he would not be disappointed.

Mary decided to ask Charles for his reactions not as a newspaper man but as an individual. After all, Charles had witnessed Elvis's entire career from the rocket start to the tragic end; he must have some thoughts. Both were from the South and similar in age surely Charles would have some stories to share.

Charles laughed at the request but still gave her an answer.

"I'm not what you would consider a typical fan; I'm afraid there won't be much of a story with me. The real story is going to be with his fan, those who tended to worship the man and his music; you know the fans who considered him larger than life. Not your healthiest view of anyone especially a rock star".

Mary continued her efforts telling him he did say to talk to the traditional and nontraditional fan.

Charles responded; "I guess I did, well I do have my share of Elvis records and I enjoyed his music. I've been fortunate enough to see a few of his concerts".

Mary interrupted him telling him he sounded like a fan. Laughing;

Charles said he saw a big difference from those who enjoyed Elvis's talents to those who became obsessed with him. He then added; you couldn't be his age and not have been affected by his music or film career he was everywhere. Gathering his thoughts, Charles began to tell of the last time he had seen Elvis in concert.

"The wife and I saw him in Vegas a couple of years back and let me tell you it was quite a show we witness some true fan worship. He was such an entertainer. The man controlled the stage and the crowd it was as if he could control life itself. But sadly, appearances can be fooling. I'm afraid death is the great equalizer, and even the famous can't cheat death. No one could have predicted Elvis would die so young and in such a fashion."

As he spoke he picked up a stack of the reports and repeated his statement; "death was indeed the great equalizer no one can avoid death."

Charles returned to his recollections of Elvis telling her;

"Once we even had a pet dog named Presley. My father brought the kids a special gift, a gray tick hound puppy. Not sure why Dad felt the kids needed a dog. But one day he showed up at the house with this lovable puppy.'

Charles began to laugh adding; "Since it was just a hound dog we named him Presley and as the song says he was *nothing but a hound dog*."

Mary smiled telling Charles that it seemed he indeed had a story and asked what became of Presley.

"Unfortunately, Presley and Elvis had more in common than a name they both meet death at an early age."

Charles went on to speak of Elvis's movie career. "I'm not sure how many movies he made, but it seems I saw them all most at the Circle G drive in back in Burlington. Fun senseless movies that helped make Elvis a generational star."

Mary realized this was the impact Elvis had on the people you may not consider yourself a fan and yet you would still have a memory to share.

Mary knew everyone would have something to say about the death. She felt she would find those who lived every high and low of Elvis's career as if it were their own. People who cried the day he left for the Army and celebrated his return home when discharged. Elvis had fans of all ages, nationalities, and races and their story is what she needed to capture.

After a few moments of silence, Charles said. Personally, he felt Elvis's may have been a victim of his on popularity adding,

"If you think about it when your life is continually dissected and controlled by those in public, it can be more than a little taxing. Think about it if we had to live under such scrutiny, it would be a hell of a challenge."

Mary brought up Elvis's weight problems and asked Charles if he felt it could have been contributing factor to his death. Charles then pointed out the first rule of journalism she should not let her personal feeling influence the story. Charles wanted her to play nice and let the good folks of Dublin have their say. He assured her there would be enough speculation of the death without them contributing to it. She promised not only would she be nice, but she would be the consummate professional. She thanked him once again for the opportunity assuring him she would file a story he would be proud to have in the paper.

To Mary, the news was rather surreal as she glanced over the wire reports. She didn't know the entertainment world without Elvis. He had been at the top of the music industry nearly her entire life.

The reports stated that Elvis had been pronounced dead at Memphis Baptist Hospital at 3:30 PM at the age of 42. Restating the obvious Elvis was the king of rock n roll, touching the lives of thousands with his music and films. For nearly 25 years he had been part of the music industry well over half his life and all of Mary's. Elvis had lived most of his life in full view of thousands of adoring and demanding fans. Mary once again thought that the pressure of his career and the lifestyle could have easily been a factor in his early death. Even two years in the Army could not remove Elvis from the public stage. He was an American rock n roll icon, living under the scrutiny of an adoring public.

One of the news clipping said Elvis was given the Grammy for lifetime achievement in 1971 at the age of 36, by the National Academy of Recording Arts and Sciences of the United States. Mary felt this was strange most lifetime achievement awards were dulled out to those in the twilight of their careers, not during it, the award spoke volumes about the impact Elvis's career had on the recording industry and his fans. He helped pave the way for others as his crossover success appealed to all racial and social, economic groups. He entertained everyone with ease, but now it appears it was easier to entertain than it was to live.

As she continued to read the reports, Mary learned that Elvis was not responsive to emergency technician's efforts to revive him. Calling for the ambulance after Elvis was discovered lying on the bathroom floor at his Graceland home. Ginger Alden, Elvis's fiancé, found him and immediately summoned Al Strada Elvis's road manager to the bathroom. Fearing the worst, they called the ambulance. The ambulance rushed Elvis to Baptist Memorial Hospital, where the emergency room was petitioned off, and a team of specialist tried in vain to revive him. When the medical staff stopped their efforts, they determined Elvis had been dead for several hours. The official announcement made at 3:30 PM CST. They discovered Elvis in a pool of his vomit lying on the bathroom floor with his pajama bottoms pulled down around his ankles. As Mary read this she couldn't help but feel sorry for him and his millions of fans, after all, this was not a death fit for a king. No one would find comfort in learning Elvis had found death in such a disturbing manner.

Elvis was mortal and unfortunately too many this would be unacceptable. Mary made mental notes for her column and felt there would be no real benefit in sharing how they discovered Elvis; the information would come out it just didn't need to come from her.

Mary found it interesting the Paramedics were not alarmed when called to the mansion. They had responded to several calls in the past usually for over excited fans a few who pass out once they saw Elvis. Unfortunately, this trip proved to be the most sobering with the realization it was Elvis who needed the attention. Something else intrigued Mary the cause of death was from natural causes. She wondered how they could be sure without an autopsy. Mary returned to Charles office to see if he had any thoughts on why the cause of death would already be determined. Charles had not seen that, but it was his understanding that if natural causes are the reason for the death, it is no longer a public matter. And when it is no longer a public matter it's up to the family to request an autopsy or not, and with no obligation to do so. Charles added that maybe the physician who made the ruling was trying to conceal some information from a demanding public, but he hoped that wasn't the case.

Mary had to remind herself that Elvis was a public figure and there would be rumors and innuendos running rampant. Identifying natural causes may have been an effort to save the family some unmerited stress. Another report indicated no evidence of foul play.

The county sheriff with jurisdiction over Graceland was emphatic in that the cause of death was due to a cardiac arrhythmia or an irregular heartbeat thus the natural causes ruling. The sheriff also reported there was no evidence of drug involvement. The sheriff made this declaration even though the toxicology reports had not been completed and would not be available for some time. Charles told Mary he might just be trying to get ahead of the rumor mill. For years, people speculated Elvis had developed an addiction to pain pills and other narcotics due to an assortment of medical problems along with his chronic back pain.

The wire service printer was working overtime with stories of the death. The news was prompting an emotional tsunami as the public became aware; an outcry of love and sadness was engulfing Elvis's fans everywhere. Shock and disbelief were the rules of the day.

Mary had never witnessed anything like it. If she was going to cover the emotions of Dublin she needed to leave the wire reports alone and get to the hospital. She was captivated with the reports much like witnessing a train wreck she couldn't turn away, but this wreck was someone's life. She was now in the midst of a fascinating story; she needed to report on not read.

Mary would cover the reaction in Dublin giving a national story a local twist. Mary's excitement continued to grow she had a chance to do some real reporting it would be her biggest by-line to date. It was an assignment that would be read and talked about for years to come. She had an opportunity to demonstrate her skills as a reporter while covering history. It was a dream assignment. Mary grabbed a notebook and was off to the hospital.

On her way to the hospital, Mary began to reflect on the life of Elvis Presley. It was still hard to believe Elvis was dead. Elvis had risen to the pentacle of success he was the King of Rock N Roll; how could he be dead. Charles was right death is a great equalizer and knows no favorites, and Elvis was far from immune no matter how bright his star shined.

No warning, no indications just the news surprising everyone and the circumstances of his death made it more difficult to accept it was almost inconceivable. Mary had written obits for a few 40-year-olds, but all the deaths had been the results of accidents or terminal illnesses, but Elvis had died of natural causes at the age of 42.

Though Mary was not a big fan, she did respect the man and his accomplishments. You could easily appreciate his talent and showmanship. Mary had seen a few of his movies mostly on television. Fun, non-threatening family friendly movies. She also had a few of his records most handed down from her parents. She understood his star power and the reach of his career.

One of Mary's favorite memories was how her older brother Bryant would impersonate Elvis as a small child. Many young children tried to emulate Elvis with his swaying hips and rocking knees, and Bryant was no exception. Holding a toy guitar, he would blare out his best rendition of *Don't Step on my Blue Suede Shoes*. The impersonation had little to do with the singing it was more about how he moved his hips back and forth. He had learned the moves by watching Elvis on Television. Mary's parents would egg him own, and he loved the attention as he entertained for family gatherings and dinner parties. His cute act always brought a laugh. Later it became a source of embarrassment for him. Mary would often tell Bryant's dates they should ask him to do his Elvis impersonation, just another reason to keep your kid sister away. Thinking of him shaking his hips and playing his toy guitar still made Mary smile. Bryant's act was fun, but it also illustrated Elvis's influence.

Mary began thinking of a trip she and a group of college friends took in June to Mobile Alabama to see Elvis in Concert. Debbie Butler, a sorority sister an avid Elvis fan, convince the group to go, telling them it would be a good way to kick off summer after graduation.

Now just ten weeks later she was preparing to write about the man's death. Debbie was a huge fan suffering under unmercifully kidding about her love for Elvis. She had even decorated her room with his photos and movie posters. Debbie had seen him in concert many times and proclaimed he was one of the greatest entertainers of all time. Mary also knew if Debbie had not been such a good friend, she would have never have gone to Mobile for the show. Mary considered calling Debbie to console her as well as get her reaction.

The Mobile show did give Mary a new appreciation for Elvis's talents and showmanship the way he easily interacted with the audience. Elvis was captivating wearing his trademark sequins jumpsuit. Even with his weight problems he still made quite an impression. His appearance was very different from what she remembered from TV and his album covers. He looked bloated and unhealthy, but she never would've dreamed he would be dead so soon. Though his weight and profuse sweating were distracting his talent was evident, and one couldn't avoid getting caught up in the show. He had such a wonderfully smooth sound singing hit after hit showing some of his trademarks moves making many a fan swoon. He certainly loved his fans especially the ladies in the front row, and this made it even more, entertaining. Though, only on stage for little over an hour, he gave a memorable performance. When the show concluded, Mary heard some grumbling about its brevity, and Debbie even said she felt the show was shorter than most. But it was a show Mary would remember for quite some time.

On the drive to the hospital, Mary began listening to WDGA a local radio station hoping to catch any updated information. Billy Donald, the afternoon DJ, was playing a makeshift tribute to Elvis. He was taking calls and playing songs. The songs were only part of the entertainment the callers offered the most entertainment. Donald's listening audience were calling in expressing shock and more than a few shedding tears. On her short trip to the hospital, Mary heard some wild if not crazy calls. The sane callers shared personal stories of how Elvis had impacted their lives over the years. One lady's story was how she and her husband went on their first date to see *Jail House Rock* so Elvis would always remain special to her. But the crazy ones were the most entertaining by far.

The most bizarre of the crazies was a call from a lady named Doris; Doris was trying to make a connection between Elvis untimely death and the death of Jesus. To Donald's credit, he patiently listened as she told how Elvis had affected many lives through his music and Jesus affected lives through his teaching, even saying she felt the real similarity was how each appealed to the common man. Hearing this Mary just shook her head. She wondered how Donald could maintain his composure with such claims. Donald thanked her for the call and without comment went straight into playing Return to Sender.

Mary had to smile; Donald had opened a can of worms when he decided to take calls. The magnitude of the news was playing out throughout Dublin on the local airways in the homes and the cities businesses. Emotions were running high and somewhat irrational. All the callers had good things to say about Elvis as they tried to understand the death. One speculated that Elvis was in a better place and he would be joining his mother; telling Donald how much Elvis loved his mother. The reverence the callers held for Elvis impressed Mary. The callers supported the magnitude of the story. When Mary stopped for a red light, she made a note to call Donald later.

THE IMPACT

Mary felt things at County General, seemed a little busier than usual with several groups, milling around out front of the hospital. Mary had little doubt that the topic of discussion was the death of Elvis. It was the main topic of conversation throughout Dublin and rest of the County.

Mary recognized a few of the nurses near the entrance some looked to have been praying or crying she wasn't sure which. Mustering all her Journalism 101 skills, she approached Beverly Smith. Beverly was a charge nurse in ICU and a friend of Mary's. She was in her early 40's a little overweight but very sweet and tentative to her patients and friends. Beverly was one of Mary's first contacts at the hospital, they also attended church together, as a native of Dublin Beverly was well connected.

Though Mary knew the answer, she asked anyway. Wanting to know if Beverly had heard about Elvis's death. Beverly, looked as if she had already shed a few tears forced a smile and said she and the others were just talking about the death saying no one could believe he was gone. Beverly said;

"We are all stunned by the news, do you have any additional information?"

Mary told her;

"You probably know as much as I do. I understand his finance found him lying face down in the bathroom. Not the way you want to find anyone much less your fiancé."

Beverly agreed it certainly wasn't the way she hoped to go out. Mary informed her that the preliminary reports speculated he could have died from an irregular heartbeat. Then told her, she had come to the hospital in hopes of getting the public's reaction for the *Journa*l.

"Charles feels the death will stir up emotions and that's the angle he wants me to take on my report. And you know Charles feels there is no better place to get a public reaction than the hospital."

They both shared a laugh at Charles and his notions. Soon Beverley began sharing her thoughts on the news telling Mary;

"I've been a fan my whole life the news is just depressing. His music helped define my life. I've got more than a few of his records loved his movies and had seen him in concert a few times."

She was a fan there was no denying that. Mary asked; if Beverly could share what it was about Elvis that made her such a fan. Beverly took a moment to answer and then said;

"It was his ability to touch your heart while being incredibly sexy. He possessed a special quality enhanced by his boyish good looks and rebel spirit. That combination worked for me and a lot of others. There will never be another Elvis."

Beverly's sadness began to return as tears reappeared. Mary wondered how one could be so emotional over someone she had never met only knowing him through a well-constructed image? Mary was fascinated by the emotional connections individuals make with people they never really know. Beverly showed all the signs of dealing with an emotional challenge brought on by the death of a family member not that of an entertainer. Maybe Mary was too judgmental, not understanding the emotions of others and how vulnerable some could be.

Before going inside, Mary spoke to a few of the others. The reactions were the same, total disbelief and sadness. Once inside the hospital, Mary decided her first stop would be the hospital pharmacy. Walking into the lobby, Mary encountered more distraught fans wearing their emotions like a badge of honor. It was difficult to understand the emotional side show. The pharmacy located on the first floor is where Mary found Andy Gaster, the pharmacist. Gaster said he couldn't remember every seeing any event quite like this more than a few people were stunned and having some difficulty accepting the news. Gaster then told her he had filled a few orders for sedatives not certain the demand had anything to do with the news. He wasn't sure what the emotional reaction said about the mental framework of the community. Gaster was far from a fan when he describes Elvis as an overweight out of touch entertainer, adding he was an entertainer, not the president. Mary smiled and told Gaster she was having some of the same feelings but had been afraid to voice them. She hoped the reaction they were witnessing was just the initial shock and as the news sinks in things would begin returning to normal. Gaster agreed, hoping she was right.

Mary's next stop was administration. The work day was coming to an end, but a few employees remained at their desk. The administrative staff appeared to be dealing with Elvis's death a little more rational. At the front desk, Susan Boss was listening to the Billy Donald show. Mary committed that Donald had quite a situation on his hands with the callers. Susan agreed Donald had opened a can of worms that he may wish he had left undisturbed. Mary said; "some of the callers I heard make me think I should do a piece on them if nothing else it would surely be entertaining." Susan acknowledged there would be plenty to write about adding there were more than a few nuts calling the show. Mary had to ask if Susan heard the lady comparing Elvis to Jesus and with that Susan just rolled her eyes and told Mary after all they were in the south.

Mary soon saw Gary Jackson the hospital administrator standing outside his office. When he noticed Mary, he laughed saying "so the *Journal* wants the hospital's view on the death of Elvis." Gary was always polite, but he could also be a little flirtatious as well. Several years her senior Mary still found his flirtatious side flattering more friendly that intrusive. Mary responded that there seemed to be a story that needed some attention and she was the one to do it. Gary said;

"I know you will be successful all I ask is for you to be respectful to whomever you talk. You'll have little trouble getting Dublin's reaction the challenge may lie in what to write. From what I've seen it's a national story playing out on everyone's doorstep."

Mary like his description and told him she might have to use it. Gary just grinned and said he was always there for her and glad to be of service.

Gary wondered if Mary had drawn the short straw or if Charles was expanding the obituary department to include rock stars? Mary couldn't hide her pleasure with the assignment, telling Gary, Charles had searched for just the right reporter and well she just happened to be the only one in the office. Right, place right time and a little luck. Mary informed him she had already visited the pharmacy and yes there was a story to be told, and she hoped to write an article Charles and the citizens of Dublin would find acceptable. Gary then said:

"I would think the assignment will be somewhat like walking on egg shells, you need to be careful, but you also need to break a few eggs to make an omelet. (*Laughing*), if it doesn't work out, you're still young, and I feel certain the paper would give you another chance."

Mary just smiled and exited the office.

Her next stop was the cafeteria where the smell of the night's special salmon patties and rice filled the air. She hoped to interview a few employees and visitors. But for the most part, the reactions were the same. People spoke of how they would miss Elvis with many reflecting on some favorite memories. Mary began to realize the story was far greater than a group of middle-aged women in mourning; the real story would be in the way the country responds to the death of a living legend. Elvis's death was touching many, and the emotional impact had no boundaries. Elvis was leaving a void that would be felt in Dublin as well as the world of entertainment. Mary began to fantasize this could be the break she desired. Do a good job and who knows what the future would hold?

Before Mary headed back to the office, she decided to visit Gary Jackson's office once again and thank him for the hospitality. She located him in his office and offered up a flirtatious statement;

"I see I'm not the only one working late."

Jackson smiled telling her; "If you came around here more in the evening, you would know this is standard behavior."

Both laughed and then Gary asked:

"How did the interviews go?"

"I'm happy to announce things seemed to be returning to normal maybe the shock of the news was wearing off."

Gary said; "that was one of the advantages of working here you can't linger on the past for long there will always be something needing your attention."

They were sharing some small talk of the community's reaction when Gary stated the obvious telling her the real story is in Memphis. Adding that's where she should be. Mary said she could only imagine what must be happening in Memphis that would be a great story, but she did work for the *Journal,* not the *Constitution* and was just happy having this assignment. Gary told her if she couldn't go to Memphis maybe he could bring Memphis to her. Mary wondered how he hoped to do that.

Gary smiled saying he had his ways. As it turns out, County General was managed by a group out of Memphis the Regional Health Care Group. And luckily for her, the District Vice President was in town for business and was a native of Memphis. Allan Conrad had flown in that morning and would be flying back later that night. Gary said maybe he could arrange for her to meet with him for a short while. Allen had lived in Memphis his entire life, and Gary felt maybe Conrad could give her more information about her assignment. Mary couldn't agree more she loved the prospect of speaking to someone with a Memphis connection. She promised Jackson she would not take up too much of his time. Gary felt Conrad would be flattered to do the interview. Mary knew if she were able to interview someone from Memphis would be icing on the cake for a great assignment. Her day was turning out to be very special.

Gary took Mary to a back office where she saw a gentleman seated at a desk working. Gary then said, "Allen, if you have a few minutes I have someone here who would love to speak to you if possible." Almost immediately Conrad rose from the desk and extended his hand saying hello to Mary and gave his name. She smiled introduced herself, and before she could tell him anymore, Gary spoke up.

"Mary here is Dublin's own Lois Lane and she is writing a piece for our paper on the death of Elvis I thought you might be able to help her out, you know give her a Memphis slant."

Mary quickly insisted; "I'm no Lois Lane, but I sure would love to talk with you about Elvis. That is if you have the time".

He told her it would be his pleasure and asked her to have a seat and to please call him Allan. Mary took a seat and once again thanked him for the opportunity. Conrad was a distinguished looking man of about 50 with a nice smile that made him appear somewhat younger.

Mary wasn't sure where to begin. She started out with an open question. She wondered how he felt the city of Memphis would be dealing with the news. Conrad looked at the ceiling contemplating his answer telling her;

"I'm sure it is something to behold. Elvis was loved and had always been a solid ambassador for the city. I feel certain the city is awash in emotions."

She then asked him for his thoughts on Elvis. He took a minute before answering;

"I've always felt Elvis had two identities he was an international star, and he was a small-town boy who loved his family. For him, problems arose when the two identities collided. Tell you the truth I've felt for a while that Elvis's life had become a tug of war between those identities. Elvis needed the stardom to support his lifestyle and family, but he longed for the simple life he knew as a boy. That's just the amateur psychologist in me coming out."

Conrad then told Mary he had spoken to his wife earlier and she said officials were predicting close to three hundred thousand fans would be coming to Memphis for the funeral. Adding Elvis had lived in Memphis his entire life, he could only imagine how people would be taking the news. Conrad said his wife Annette informed him the local news is already referring to the funeral as Elvis's last public appearance. Mary thought a public appearance no one wanted or could believe.

Conrad said one thing for certain Memphis would never forget its favorite son. Mary wondered if Conrad's wife had any information on the funeral. She did not it seemed there was a great deal of speculation but no details.

After a few minutes talking about the death and Memphis's reaction, Conrad made an offer that surprised Mary. He told her if she wanted to know what was going on in Memphis, she should consider flying back with him later that night Mary couldn't believe he was serious and laughed it off saying it would be tempting. Sensing her disbelief, he assured her there was plenty of room on the plane. And if she was inclined, he could have her in Memphis covering the story firsthand. Jackson overheard the proposal and told Mary she should consider it. The offer would put her smack in the middle of the action adding it would also be great for the *Journal*. Conrad in making the offer told her not only would she be in the middle of the story but he would welcome the company. Mary loved the idea of covering one of the biggest stories of the year but also being able to witness it. Her article would come from her interviews and the experiences she would encounter in Memphis.

It was an inviting offer. Mary looked at both men in questioning disbelief. Asking Conrad if he was serious. Conrad assured her he was. Gary then added;

"Mary, not more than an hour ago, you'd talked about how great this assignment was. And the only thing that would make it better would be covering it in Memphis, and now you have a chance."

Conrad told her he could get her to Memphis getting home would be up to her. Mary's desire to be in Memphis over road any worry she may have of getting home. Mary began to consider the offer. She found it very exciting and could only imagine what being in Memphis would mean.

To Mary, it was a chance to test her spirit as well as her journalistic skills. She had never been much on spontaneity, but since leaving college she had decided to take more risk, and this certainly was a risk. Flying to Memphis with a man she didn't know may be a little riskier than she wanted. But she saw something in Allan Conrad that was reassuring and trustworthy. Other than her fear of the unknown she couldn't come up with an argument against the offer. She had little to lose. Her old self would have turned down the offer, but the new Mary saw an opportunity. She ran the scenario over in her head, and each time something told her to go. She would have a personal look behind the curtain of one of the biggest stories of the year. Even if it meant venturing into the unknown, she decided to take Conrad up on his offer. Mary said if he were serious she would like to join him. Gary smiled and said that was the Lois Lane attitude we know and love. Mary then pointed out there was one caveat before she could fully commit she needed to get approval from her editor. A no from him would be a deal killer. Gary offered to talk to Charles, but Mary knew she needed to be the one doing the negotiating. Mary didn't feel Charles would object and her being in Memphis would give the paper an eye witness to the funeral. But she also knew how crazy the trip sounded and could count on Charles to have some valid questions and may even see things differently.

Mary asked how much time she had. Conrad told her. Unfortunately, he had work that still needed some attention, but he hopes to be able to leave around 8:30. She now had nearly two hours to prepare. Conrad told her if she could clear it with her editor he would plan on seeing her at the airport later. He told her the plane was at the AirCorp hanger and wondered if she knew where that was. Mary was confident she could find it. Gary gave her the phone number for the hanger and instructed her to call if she was detained or couldn't make it. Mary told them she thought she could pull it off.

Mary felt Charles would see the many advantages to having a reporter in Memphis it would be quite a feat for a small-town paper. Though she was the new kid in town, she was confident she could handle the assignment. The more she thought about it, the greater her excitement. She would be covering a national story impacting the world, not just Dublin. It was the type of assignment she dreamed of in school, and now it could be a reality, she would be able to do some real journalism.

Knowing there is no better time than the present Mary decided to call Charles from the hospital. She asked Gary if she could use a phone. Gary directed Mary to an empty office allowing her to have some privacy for the call. Before making the call, Mary ran over in her head how she would approach Charles. Figuring she would offer to pay her expenses and he could consider reimbursing her after he read the story no strings attached she was willing to take the chance if he was.

Charles was still at the office picking up the phone after two rings. Mary took a long deep breath and began her sell. She told Charles; 'I was hoping to catch you."

Charles said he was waiting to hear from her. Naturally, he wondered how the interviews were going. She gave him a quick update and then added she had a question for him. Before Charles could respond, she asked how he would feel about having a reporter in Memphis covering the story firsthand. Recognizing a trick question when he heard one he naturally said he would love that. Mary then told Charles he might need an open mind for what she was about to suggest, and she wanted him to give it some thought. She then began telling him of Conrad's offer. Mary was now very enthusiastic she wasn't sure what surprised Charles more the offer or her willingness to go. Charles was naturally a little hesitant about the trip and began asking her questions as to what she hoped to get accomplished. He wanted to make sure she had thought it through. Asking such questions as did she have a place to stay and how long she would be gone? Things she hadn't even considered. Mary answered his concerns the best way she knew, telling him. Those were fair questions, and she sure understood his concern, but she couldn't help but feel this was a good opportunity for her and the paper and she could figure it all out once she got there. She assured Charles she could handle it and was excited about the challenge.

Mary knew Charles was showing concern after all he had children close to her in age and the parent in him was coming out. Mary recognized it sounded a bit crazy but felt it was something she needed to and wanted to do. Charles laughed saying he could tell she was serious, and if she felt she can handle it then who was he to say no.

Charles gave his blessings, only requesting she return as soon as possible to file the story, and for God's sake be careful and be smart. She thanked him and said she would. Charles told her to go and bring back an award-winning article. Though Charles had some mixed feeling about the trip, she felt the journalist in him won over his parental side. Before hanging up, he told her if she needed anything just let him know but hopefully, she wouldn't need anything.

The reality was beginning to sink in, and Mary began to wonder what the next few days would bring. Hanging up the phone, she took another deep breath and made her way back into Gary's office. Gary and Conrad were still talking when they looked up and smiled wondering the verdict. Her smile gave them the answer and Conrad said it looked like he would have some company on the flight back. Both men seemed pleased. Gary said, "I thought Charles would be okay with it." Mary told him; "it did take a little persuasion, but in the end, he gave me his blessing." Trying not to show her nervousness she told them she would see them at 8:30. Gary said; "remember Aircorp hanger you can park to the left of the building your car will be safe there." She thanked them once again smiling as she exited the room.

Time was of the essence she left the hospital and drove straight to the office hoping to tie up a few things before going home to pack. There was the obituary she needed to finish, and she also wanted to construct a small article on the death for tomorrow's edition of the paper.

Back in her office, she found writing the short article to be a little more challenging than it should have been, her excitement prevented her from concentrating. While attempting to make sense out of her notes, Terrie Mann, a senior reporter called. Terrie told Mary she was hoping to catch her before she left. Charles had called her looking for some reassurance on his decision supporting her trip. Mary told her; "I feel Charles was thinking as a father, not an editor, but the paper won out in the end." Terrie said; "that's Charles he's protective of everyone." Terri wanted to know Mary's side of the story. Even though Mary knew Terri was supportive, she was still little apprehensive as she explained how the trip came about and what she hoped to do. Terrie gave her an encouraging good for you, telling her it sounded as if she had a plan. Assuring her not everyone gets this kind of opportunity and she should take full advantage of it. Terri then expressed her envy of Mary being in the middle of a major news story. Mary hoped she was right adding that she wanted to look back on it years from now as a pleasant memory not one of horror.

Terrie told her;

"Your feelings are only natural, but I'm betting on you. I'm sure you will have a great time. Listen I know you are pressed for time leave your notes, and I'll take care of tomorrow's story."

Mary was relieved to hear Terri's offer knowing she wasn't getting much done. Terrie then told her she was sure Mary would learn a lot about herself and her profession. Terri confirmed it was the right thing to do not allowing fear to win out over excitement adding she knew Mary would do great. Terrie suggested Mary check out a camera to get some photos and then said she wished she was going with her. Mary thanked her for the support.

Soon Mary returned to the task at hand she had a lot to get done before leaving and certainly didn't want to get left behind. She compiled her notes adding a few ideas for the story and placed them on Terrie's desk. She also scribbled a thank you note telling her she would get an exclusive over lunch once she returned. On her way, out she secured a camera, and four rolls of film and grabbed a couple of legal pads. Mary didn't take the time to speak to anyone else in the building knowing she had a lot to get done. She did, however, reflect on how lucky she was. She not only had a great opportunity to go to Memphis but she was fortunate to be working with a wonderful group of people.

The clock was ticking Mary created a mental checklist of things she needed. Get money, pack clothes, and let her roommate Sherrie know what she was doing. Sherrie would surely think it was a crazy idea.

Mary stopped by a local grocery and cashed a check before going home to pack. Sherrie wasn't home so Mary wrote a quick note saying she was fine and had decided to go to Memphis to cover Elvis's funeral asking her not to worry and she would explain later.

THE FLIGHT

DRIVING TO THE AIRPORT, MARY once again listened to WDGA. Regular programming had returned, and Mary imagined Billy Donald was getting a drink somewhere recovering from his makes shift call-in show. As the music played Mary began to consider some of Charles's questions; how would she handle the assignment and where would she stay, how would she, get around town. She had few answers but for some reason wasn't worried thinking only of the adventure. Dublin's airport seemed deserted. The airport's primary function was to serve private aircraft owners, so Mary had little trouble locating the hanger at the small airport once parked all she could do was smile as she exited her car she knew it was time to shine.

Mary had a mental picture of airport scene out of Casablanca and the words; *this could be the beginning of a wonderful relationship*. Her life like the lives of those in the movie would be changing forever once she boarded the plane. It was decision time if she had any hesitations now was the time. She had no indecision grabbing her bags and began walking toward the front of the hanger. Turning the corner of the hanger, she spotted Gary and Conrad; they appeared to be engaged in a lively conversation. With a bit of nervousness, she announced her presence. Both men smiled as she walked up. Mary tried to conceal her nervousness telling them she hoped they hadn't been waiting long. Gary told her no they had just gotten there themselves.

Mary then noticed how small the plane was. She didn't know what to expect but was hoping for a little larger plane. Saying loudly "is that the plane." Gary laughing told her;

"There's still time to change your mind."

"No, I'm going maybe not as enthusiastically as earlier, but I'm going."

The plane was a two-engine Cessna slick in appearance but still seemed rather small compared to other planes; Mary had flown in. Beige in color with detailed striping giving it a sleek appearance. Conrad told her not to let first impressions fool her it's a great plane and she should be quite comfortable. Mary hoped he was right. Conrad said the flight would be a little over two hours and promised she would hardly know she was in the air.

Conrad called over a man checking out the plane introduced him as Mike Coley, the pilot. Mike said he understood Mary would be accompanying them back to Memphis? Coley looked younger than his years Conrad even said; don't let his youthful appearance fool you, he's an excellent pilot with a lot of experience. She told him it wasn't Mike who worried her. Mike laughed and said;

"The plane may be small, but I assure you it's safe and top of the line I'm certain you will enjoy the flight."

Gary jokingly added other than a few barrel rolls it should be a calm flight. Coley told him not to spoil the fun and share all his secrets. Mary laughed telling them they could stop now she was not going to change her mind. It was then Conrad said; "let's get this party started." Mike picked up Mary's bag and said he believed she had a funeral to cover.

Before boarding the plane Mary hugged Gary, telling him she

would see him in a few days. Conrad shook Gary's hand telling him not to worry about Mary she was in good hands. Gary said; "it's Memphis I'm worried about." Everyone was laughing, Mary's may have been nervous laughter, but it didn't take away from her excitement. She felt the next few days would be challenging but also exciting. Mary knew a great adventure awaited her. Mary's father use to tell the children life is full of challenges, and it's what you do with those challenges that determine the person you become. Take your challenge head on give it your best effort and good things will happen. She knew this was one of those times.

Once Mary was on board, she could see how nice the plane was. Mary thought it had a new car smell clean and invited. Taking her seat, Mary immediately pulled out her notebook. Conrad soon joined her taking the seat facing her with his back to the pilot. Coley was making last minute inspections before loading the luggage. Once he climbed on and began bulking his seatbelt Mary again was confronted with the reality of her decision. Mary just smiled knowing many of her friends would say she had lost her mind. She was confident she'd made the right decision. She was preparing to cover the funeral of the year if not the decade. Elvis Presley was a cultural icon, and Mary would be present for his last public appearance. Leaning back to make herself comfortable the song *"If they could see me now"* began running through her head. Yea if they could see her now that old gang, oh what would they say?

Coley appeared to be talking to himself as he began to flip levers and check gauges. Soon the engines began to roar. The airfield was clear as they started taxing down the runway. Conrad said "it looks like a beautiful night for a flight," Mary just smiled in agreement a smile that would not leave her face anytime soon. Coley looked back at them saying, No lines no waiting they were preparing to taxi down the runway. There was no backing out now Coley said if everyone's buckled in, let's do this. Mary was fascinated with the speed of the props as the plane moved toward lift-off. Soon the plane lifted into the air, and Conrad grinned saying we have lift off. Mary had a perfect view of Dublin as Twilight was about to be replaced with darkness it was a beautiful sight

As she looked over the city of Dublin, she contemplated the adventure that lied ahead. She still didn't know where she would stay or how she would get around, but now that seemed trivial. Soon Coley told them they could loosen their seatbelts adding all systems were go for an uneventful fight. Mary knew when it came to flying the term uneventful was a good thing.

Where had, this adventurous side come from she had never been one to be so adventurous. But here she was on her way to Memphis with two men who less than three hours ago, were complete strangers. Dear Lord where did she get the idea that this was a smart move. The assignment in Dublin was one thing but going to Memphis geez that's crazy. And now she is high over Georgia in a plush puddle jumper. She was embarking on an adventure not covered in journalism school.

Conrad must have sensed her thoughts asking if she had any regrets. Mary told him she was just trying to take it all in. He reassured her things would be fine adding she should try to relax she was going to need her rest.

Soon Conrad pulled down a tray from what appeared to be a small bar substituted for a seat. He said he was going to have a drink and wonder if she wanted to join him. "Why not," damn she was taking on a new persona adding drinking to the flight her mind must have been taken over by aliens. Conrad said; "I can offer you some of Tennessee's finest whiskey or if you prefer we have a small selection of sodas." Her adventurous side had taken control, and she asked for a small glass of the Tennessee whiskey with a little ginger ale. As Conrad prepared the drinks he told her; "I'm afraid the food selection are a bit limited." Smiling Conrad then produced a small bag of chips and a can of mixed nuts. As he handed her the drink, they toasted the flight and funeral. Mary found the drink to be just what the doctor ordered. As she sipped on the drink, her nerves began to calm. Pure excitement replaced her tension. The drink was relaxing her busy mind had finally slowed down, and she turned her attention to finishing up her interview with Conrad.

Mary wanted to learn more about Memphis and what she should expect. He began to give her a mini-course on the history of the city.

"You will find Memphis has a proud history known for its music to its Bar B Q. The music scene has a rich tradition especially in Jazz and Soul a must stop Beale Street. No matter your musical taste you'll find it on Beale St."

He assured her she would not be disappointed adding that there would be fans celebrating Elvis's career as well as mourning his death. Conrad felt the clubs would provide a good escape from the funeral activity.

"Memphis has a pretty rich history when it comes to celebrities Tennessee Williams, Johnny Cash and Cybil Sheppard all hail from Memphis."

He also reminded her of Memphis's dark history and how the assassination of Dr. Martin Luther King left a dark cloud over the city for many years. He then told her a bit of trivia;

"Memphis was once known as the Mule capital of the world, a tribute to the once flourishing mule trade. For years, the city even had a mule day celebration."

Mary laughed thinking of a mule celebration what else would she learn. She knew the funeral of Elvis would be the latest installment of the history of Memphis.

They continued to talk; Mary was enjoying the flight and the company. After a while Coley interrupted them saying they were about 30 minutes out adding he hoped they were enjoying the flight. Mary held up her glass smiling. Coley echoed Conrad's' thoughts on Memphis telling her she should enjoy herself adding the city influenced Elvis long before he influenced the city.

Turning her attention back to Conrad Mary asked if he minded sharing his feelings about Elvis. Conrad felt he couldn't add much more.

"Elvis moved to Memphis as a teenager from Tupelo Mississippi a town about 100 miles southeast of Memphis. It was a tough time for him and his family. He had to work for his success, and I'm not sure Elvis would have found success if not for the move to Memphis. Memphis is where he received his musical education. No matter the musical style Elvis experienced it."

Conrad continued to tell Mary how Elvis would sneak into some of the clubs on Beale Street hearing such acts as B. B. King or the legendary bluesman Furry Lewis. Mary wasn't familiar with Lewis. Conrad told her;

"Furry Lewis was a blues master not commercially popular but one of the greats and an early influence on Elvis's career." Personally, I feel it was his introduction to these blues artists that laid the foundation for what would become the classic Elvis style. The clubs provided only a portion of his musical influence. Supposedly Elvis spent many hours listening to the radio. Those were the golden years of radio, and he would listen to the *Grand Ole Opera* broadcast out of Nashville and *The Louisiana Hayride* out Shreveport La."

Mary was fascinated hearing about the early influences on Elvis and his music and learned that *The Louisiana Hayride*, had given Elvis one of his first opportunities to perform before a live audience. Conrad added;

"I understand the Hayride show wasn't all that good, but it did light a fire for Elvis to perform. From all the stories I've heard, I would say Elvis was a musical sponge soaking it all in, and it was this love for music that helped drive him to be successful; he loved the effect music had on him and others."

Mary learned that Elvis had other jobs, though one would think his whole life had been music. Conrad told her one of Elvis's first jobs was as a truck driver, and it was while driving a truck help lead to his discovery. As a delivery driver, Elvis heard about a small studio on Union Avenue where he could make a demo recording. For a modest fee, the hopeful artist could hear how they sounded on record. Conrad went on to say;

"The first demo was a gift for his mother. It's an urban legend that though Elvis gave the recording to his mother, the family didn't own a record player. Word is Elvis wasn't pleased with the recording. But his disappointment didn't deter him from trying again. And it was on one of his following recording session the legendary Sam Phillips discovered him. Philips owned Sun Records, and as they say, it became Rock N Roll history. Phillips was instrumental in the careers of many artists including Jerry Lee Louis and Johnny Cash. I never felt Phillips got the recognition he deserved when it came to his influence on the musical world. Phillip did it all producer a studio owner and talent scout. Phillips believed if he could find a white artist with a soulful black sound he could turn that artist into a crossover sensation for both races. And it was Elvis's soulful sound that made him a household word."

Mary questioned Conrad if Phillips still owned Sun Records.

Conrad told her, Phillips had sold the studio many years ago, Mary said; "you seem to know a lot about Elvis?" Shaking his head, he told her; "it's a result of growing up in Memphis. Elvis always called Memphis home even though he could have lived anywhere in the world, so it's only natural."

Mary then asked if Conrad could tell her anything about Graceland Elvis's home.

"I'll tell you what I know. The house itself was built by a local doctor not sure what year, but at the time many considered it a mansion. Elvis bought it around 57 shortly after recording his first big hit *"That's Alright Mama."* I read that he paid about 100,000 for the house. I remember being impressed that a singer could buy such a house. Little did I know how much money there was in singing?"

Mary learned that there are many stories to why Elvis bought Graceland but the most logical one was the home, and land could provide him some privacy. Conrad told her;

"In the early years, Elvis had problems with neighbors complaining about the traffic congestion a result of curious fans trying to see him. His old neighbors felt Elvis was more an annoyance brought on by his new-found wealth and rock n roll lifestyle. He bought Graceland to find some peace, and the home would also be a nice gift for his parents. They had never really enjoyed a secure home. In the early years before purchasing Graceland, there were plenty of curious fans including my younger brother Ricky? He and his friends would gather at the Creamery a local hang out and drive out to what was rumored to be the home of Elvis."

"Did they ever see him?"

"They often claimed to, but who knows if they ever actually did."

"The sad thing is that the more privacy he desired, the less he got. Once people learned he had bought Graceland, it just created more curiosity seekers, and now everyone knew where he lived. The oasis Elvis had hoped for became a tourist attraction, but he never moved."

Mary asked Conrad's thoughts on Elvis's career. Conrad said;

"I feel Elvis was as close to an overnight sensation as one could get. It didn't take long for his career to take off outgrowing Sun Records. To Sam Phillips credit he recognized Elvis needed to be with a larger label and sold his contract to RCA. The move to a bigger label helped introduce him to a much larger audience with better distribution."

Conrad felt you could put Elvis's career into three categories. The first was the fifties where he laid the foundation for his rock n roll persona. Then in the 60's he became a movie star, and finally, in the later years, he became an entertainer, not just a singer. The Vegas shows the TV specials all designed to show another side of his talent. Conrad felt Elvis was a once in a lifetime talent.

Mary asked had he ever seen Elvis perform. The question seemed to touch a cord with Conrad as he smiled and said;

"Plenty of times mostly in the early years. But it had been awhile, and I was as surprised as anyone with the death. The times I did see him, he had plenty of energy and stage presence. Those memories make it hard to believe he's gone."

As Coley began his descent to Memphis Mary asked Conrad if he had any suggestions for a place to stay. Conrad felt she would want to be as near Graceland as possible, and he would help her find a place. Once again Mary depended on the goodness of strangers. Conrad told her not to worry she would do fine and should have a wonderful time. Mary was glad someone had faith in her. Conrad assured her Memphis was a very friendly city and she wouldn't be alone considering the number of people coming into town to say their goodbyes. He was sure she would have quite an adventure.

Mary wondered how she could ever repay Conrad for his kindness and help. He graciously asks her to send him a copy of her story, and they could call it even adding he wanted it signed. Mary told him that was easy, but it didn't seem to be nearly payment enough. What a small price to pay for such kindness. She did have a few uncertainties about the story, after all, it was a long way from the obituary column. But if she was going to do the story justice, there was no better place to be. Soon she would be in the middle of the action making her especially thankful. Not only did she get a free flight to Memphis she had made a new friend.

Coley told them it was a beautiful night in Memphis. Mary finished the last of her drink and sat back to enjoy the landing. Soon the lights of Memphis appeared below; raising her anxiety even more. When the wheels hit the runway, and they began to taxi toward an adventure of a lifetime Mary smile.

The hanger was close to the main terminal where large windows looked out onto the runway. From what Mary, could tell there seemed to be plenty of activity. Once the plane came to a stop, Coley asked Mary if she enjoyed her flight. Mary responded, "It was great." Coley then opened the cabin door and helped Mary off the plane telling her he was glad she found the flight to her liking. She thanked him, and he simply replied "Glad to be of service." He told her he hoped her stay in Memphis would be enjoyable, and he handed her his card saying if there is anything he could help her with just give him a call.

The airport was full of life Conrad even committed about it being busier than usual adding once Mike secures the plane they would get going. Coley told them;

"Don't wait for me I've got to take care of the plane and file some paperwork."

Conrad asked; "Do you need a ride."

"No, I've got my car, I'll see you Thursday."

Mary wondered where they would be flying off to next but didn't ask. Coley once again told Mary it was a pleasure meeting her and he hoped she has a great time in Memphis. Mary thanked him as they hugged. She found the hospitality and generosity of her new friends amazing.

The terminal would give Mary her first taste of Memphis. Conrad said he had a driver who should be waiting out front; Mary thought this is the way to travel. Mary asked;

"How much traveling do you do?"

"More than I cared to admit, but sometimes I'm fortunate enough to meet interesting people like yourself."

Mary blushed a little and thanked him. He told her he should be the one thanking her he had enjoyed her company. Even with the night air being sticky, Mary enjoyed their brief walk to the terminal especially after setting so long. They walked down a covered breezeway where they reached a gate that led to the terminal. The airport was alive with activity. Conrad shook his head and told her things certainly were busier than usual, and she would have plenty of company while in Memphis. For Mary, the story was beginning, and now she had to decide what to write.

Mary's adventure was unfolding, the activity the people all would contribute to her article. She wasn't sure she could be any more excited. One of the first things to catch her attention was a souvenir stand selling Elvis paraphernalia; bumper stickers, pennants, and T-shirts you name it, and they were selling it. She thought it was strange that there were so much memorabilia available considering it had only been a few hours since the news of the death broke. Prepared or not Mary was in the middle of the action.

As they walked out of the terminal, they turned to the left toward a taxi stand where Mary noticed an older gentleman standing beside a Lincoln Continental. It was the service. Smiling the driver says "evening Mr. Conrad hope you had a nice trip." Conrad thanked him and said he did indeed and even brought someone back with him. The gentleman turned his attention to Mary and introduced himself as Thomas Hill. Adding that on behalf of the city of Memphis welcome. Mary thanked him and introduced herself as Mary McGill. Conrad informed Thomas this was Mary's first trip to Memphis; she was there to cover Elvis's funeral. Thomas asked if she was a reporter. Mary was proud to say yes, yes she was. She liked the question and liked her response better she was indeed a reporter. Thomas then said to Mary; there will be plenty to report on, the city is growing by the minute. Conrad then said the first thing they needed to do was find Mary a place to stay. Thomas smiled and said that might take a little doing; the hotels are filling up fast, but he was sure they could find something. Mary hoped he was right.

WELCOME TO MEMPHIS

A FEW OF THE HOTELS SURROUNDING the airport were already posting no vacancy. Thomas told Mary that not only were the hotel rooms being taken up by those coming in for the funeral, but there was also a National Shriners Convention taking place. Mary asked about the convention; Thomas told her it was not just a convention but the largest in the world. Shriners had been arriving since Sunday, and they were quite an interesting group, and all seemly enjoy a good party. Between the convention and funeral, it was going to be quite a week.

As they were pulling out on to the highway, Conrad suggested Thomas drive to the Holiday Inn University. That's when Mary learned something else about Memphis. Memphis was home to the corporate headquarters of Holiday Inn International. The founder of Holiday Inn was a Memphis native, and it was where he opened his first hotel. Conrad continued to talk about Holiday Inn and its history, but Mary was paying little attention hoping just to find a room. Conrad failed to pick up on her nervousness as he told her Memphis was not only the home of the first Holiday Inn but also the companies training facility known as Holiday Inn University. At the training facility, perspective managers came from all over to learn the business of managing a Holiday Inn. Once he said he was certain she could find a room Mary began to relax a bit more. Conrad said.'

"Our company does a great deal of business with them so hopefully; they can accommodate you.".

Mary felt the complex resembled little more than a large hotel. Along with being a working hotel, it was also a teaching facility. Thomas dropped them off at the front door and pulled Mary's bag from the trunk. Conrad took the bag telling Thomas they shouldn't be long. He then turned to Mary saying; "let's see what we can find." He walked her into the lobby and Mary was happy when the desk clerk a man named Brad recognized Conrad immediately.

"Mr. Conrad nice to see you what brings you out this time of night?"

"Brad I'm hoping you can help my friend the reporter" He then pointed to Mary. "She's hoping to find a room."

Mary smiled looking needy as possible. Brad looked over at her saying she was in luck they could always find room for friends of Mr. Conrad's. He pulled out a clipboard and asked her how long she would be staying. Mary told him two possible three nights adding she was there to cover Elvis's funeral. He handed her the registration and welcomed her to Memphis. Conrad extended his hand to Brad and thanked him. He then instructed Brad to take good care of Mary. Brad smiled saying he would do just that. Conrad then turned to Mary and said;

"it appears you've met two of your needs you have arrived in Memphis and now have a place to stay. You will be in good hands with Brad."

As he prepared to leave Mary gave him a huge thank you hug. Though she had only met the man, she now considered him a friend.

Conrad gave her his contact information and instructed her not to hesitate to call and then reminded her he wanted a copy of the story.

When Conrad exited the hotel lobby, Mary once again began to hum "*If they could see me now*." It was going to be her theme song. Her old crowd would have been surprised, but she was doing this, and she was going to enjoy it. As Mary was finishing her registration, she heard a gentleman asking Brad about a room. The man had a distinctive reassuring English accent. Brad told the gentleman they still had a few rooms available. Once the Englishman heard this, he expressed a sigh of relief saying the hotel rooms seemed to be going fast. Before Brad took the man's information, he handed Mary her room key telling her where to locate her room.

Mary overheard Brad tell the gentleman;

"As a rule, the hotel seldom opens up the entire hotel to the public normally most of the rooms are for employees in training. But with such demand, we decided to open everything up".

Mary was still intrigued by the gentleman's English accent she decided to introduce herself. The journalist in her wanted to see if there was a story with him and personally, she had always been a sucker for an English accent. She told him they were both lucky to find a room and with that extended her hand "Mary McGill." It was then that she noticed there was another gentleman standing at the desk. The taller of the two she imagined was in his early 40's looked at her and with his wonderful accent said Ma'am. It was then that she realized her southern accent intrigued him as much as his English brogue did her. Soon they were speaking in unison, and both were asking the same question. "Where are you from?"

They shared a laugh, and he asked; "are you in Memphis for the funeral"? The question caught her off guard. Of course, she was there to cover the funeral, but she was still somewhat insecure when it came to discussing her duties, and this was by no means a normal assignment. Just the same she told them "yes covering the funeral for my paper back home." She was surprised when he began to guess which paper she represented. He may have been flirting with her or just being polite, but he asked if she was with the *Atlanta Constitution,* or perhaps the *Miami Herald.* She was flattered by his lofty guesses, but she laughed telling him no she represented a much bigger paper she was in Memphis representing the Dublin *Journal.* That is Dublin Ga., adding; "I'm sure you've heard of it." Now, who was flirting? He had an engaging smile telling her he was not familiar with it maybe she could feel him in later. No matter his intentions she was now a victim of his English charm and accent. He then introduced himself as Roger Dixon from the *Daily Mirror* in London and introduced the man with him as a photojournalist also from the Mirror named Wayne Donald. Donald was older and not nearly as friendly. If anything, Donald seemed put off by the entire conversation. Mary told him she was impressed "The *London Mirror*" and she assumed they were in Memphis for the funeral as well. Roger said; "Yes we are hoping to the give the fine folks across the pond a rundown on how America says goodbye to a star."

Mary was feeling a bit more comfortable said maybe they could talk later, she would love to get his take on the proceedings maybe he could give a small-town girl some pointers. Roger grinned and said;

"I'm sure you are quite capable of handling the story, but it would be my pleasure to talk with you."

"Tell you what Ms. McGill, from the Dublin *Journal,* since we are here for the same reason why don't we team up."

The offer surprised Mary, but she also found it exciting. She was taken aback by his forwardness but was also pleased with the proposal. Trying to conceal her excitement she readily accepted his proposition. Roger felt it would be good to have a native with them and he would be glad to give her his thoughts on the death and funeral. She said;

"I hate to disappoint you I may not be able to give much of a local take; it's my first trip to Memphis, and Dublin Georgia is nearly 500 miles away."

Roger being ever, so the gentleman told her; "no worry in London, Georgia would be considered local." Now she knew he was flirting, and she was flattered by his attention, and she loved the request. She continued the banter telling him she was rather new at reporting and maybe she could learn some things from him. Roger then said something that resonated with her, telling her not to worry no one had ever covered the funeral of Elvis before. She liked this perspective. Though others would have more experience and additional resources, it would still be a new and unique experience for everyone. Mary extended her hand telling Roger it would be a pleasure working with him. Donald interrupted their conversation saying if the two of them had finished with the introductions maybe they could formulate a plan so he could get to the room.

Mary was curious asking them how they had gotten to Memphis so quickly the news of the death was still rather fresh. She told them she was a lot closer to Memphis than London and had just arrived. Roger made light of her southern drawl asking if she said Y'all.

"Yes, I said Y'all and Y'all be nice." Roger grinned answering, "We were already working in the states in Nashville doing a piece on the Grand Ole Opera when the news broke."

Mary learned Country Music was quite popular in the UK and the Mirror decided to do a feature on the home of country music. Once they learned of Elvis's death, all it took was a few calls, and they had a new assignment.

They moved away from the desk and continued the conversation walking toward the elevators. Roger then added; "as it turned out getting the assignment was the easy part. Planning to get to Memphis, proved to be a little more difficult." Donald who Mary wasn't sure was even listening then spoke up.

"Between securing an auto and Rogers driving."

Roger broke in; "I'm pleased to announce we were able to make it no worse for the wear."

Donald laughing told Roger that was his version. It seemed Wayne Donald had a personality, after all; maybe she had missed him. Mary's interest in working together increased once she learned they had a car. Roger said;

"Thanks to the good folks at Hertz we do have an auto. It took some doing, but we finally convinced the rental agent that we both possessed legitimate licenses and she could trust us. You probably can imagine, the poor girl who rented us the auto was a little apprehensive dealing with two English gents, she was for some reason not impressed with our UK credentials. She kept asking what side of the road we drove on. But after some delicate negotiations, they were able to obtain the auto."

Waiting for the elevator, Roger spoke to Mary;

"Ms. McGill, I'm judging from your reaction that you may have a need for an auto".

"Please call me Mary, and you're correct I don't have an auto or car for that matter. I was figuring on using a taxi, but a car would certainly make things easier."

"Mary, it seems to me, we need to be working together. We have an auto, and you need one, and we could also benefit from a good American driver."

Laughingly Donald added they could use a bad American driver.

Roger then told her he would feel better and be certain Wayne would as well if they had an American driver preferably a pretty one from Georgia. Okay, he was flirting, and he was quite charming as well. She was becoming infatuated with his charm and mannerisms. An interesting proposal and Mary liked it and once again stuck out her hand to Roger and said; "gentlemen it would be my honor to be your driver." The elevator arrived, and Mary felt as if everything was falling into place.

Mary's adrenalin was flowing, and she was wide awake summing up her nerve she asked if they were interested in going to Graceland that night. She recognized it was late but felt certain she wouldn't be able to sleep. Roger liked the idea and even stated there would be plenty of time to sleep after the funeral. Wayne added he was always up for a road trip if Roger didn't drive. They agreed there was no better time to start and decided to meet in the lobby a little later.

It had been hours since Mary had eaten and she was feeling the effects. With all the excitement and rushing around food had not been high on her list. But now she knew if she was going to survive the next few hours she needed something to eat. After settling into her room, she decided to go back down to the lobby and hopefully find something to eat while waiting on Roger and Wayne. Before leaving the room Mary instinctually turned the TV own, hoping to see if there were any new reports. One of the stations had a live feed from Graceland, judging from the shot it appeared several hundred had already arrived at the mansion. A reporter standing outside the mansion's front gate said they were anticipating close to two hundred thousand fans over the next few days.

Mary grabbed a pad and jotted down a few notes as she listens to the Graceland report. Her investigative reporting had begun. The assignment involved the death of an American recording star, but it would take some investigative work to get the story within the story. She learned President Carter and hundreds of other dignitaries had phoned the Presley home offering their condolences. President Carter had also ordered 3,000 national guardsmen sent to Memphis to help with traffic and crowd control. He was proactive wanting to address any problems before they happened.

The reporter told of the reaction of other entertainers throughout the world. Most were in shock and spoke of the many contributions Elvis had made to the music industry. The reporter also speculated on who might attend the service though the plans were still incomplete, speculation was the funeral would take place on Thursday the 18th of August. Mary hoped he was correct considering her limited time and resources. The sooner, the better. She was glad to learn the family hoped to move the body back to Graceland where Elvis would lay in state for a public viewing. It seemed everything was on the fast track as if they were rushing to get him buried. Elvis had been dead less than 24 hours, and they were already preparing a public viewing.

Before leaving for the lobby, she caught one reporter going over the next day's newspaper headlines. Probably the most revealing headline would be the one found in the Memphis Press-Scimitar the headline choice was (Lonely Life Ends on Elvis Presley Boulevard). The lonely life seemed peculiar for a man of Elvis's stature. But this reference was once again repeated in the British FrontPage declaring (King Elvis Dead at 42 and Alone). He may have been alone when he died, but he certainly wouldn't be when buried. Mary jotted down the headlines thinking she may need them later.

Between the alcohol and lack of food, Mary had a small headache, but that wasn't going to deter her. The hour may have been late, but she knew the night was young. Once back in the busy lobby, Mary felt everyone appeared to be swept up in the emotion of the day. To

Mary, it was clear Memphis's favorite son was supplying a shot to the local economy yet again. She was pleased to find the hotel grill had remained open and she could smell the burgers and fries. A quick stop for food was in order. She learned the grill had decided to extend their hours of operation due to demand, a wise business decision.

She located a table in the rear of the grill and ordered the Memphis burger supposedly the house special, (a hamburger with barbecue sauce) and a coke. Before taking her order, the waitress asked if she was here for the funeral. Mary explained to her she was there as a reporter. Mary sensing the waitress was a fan added she felt fortunate her job would give her a chance to say goodbye to the king.

It was obvious the question on everyone's lips was, "Are you here for the funeral?" And most of the answers were the same nearly everyone at the hotel had come to Memphis for the funeral. People from all walks of life had been brought together by the death of a star. The only other group was the Shriners who appeared to have their separate agenda. Mary asked the waitress if they were always this busy. The waitress said;

"Heavens no. Normally we are closed at this time of night. With so many people at the hotel, management decided to stay open. Business has been good for my pocketbook but not my feet. The funeral is bringing them in everyone I've waited on in the last couple of hours has been here for the funeral. It is going to be quite an event."

Mary told her; I can only imagine. I've felt like I've been riding a roller coaster since hearing the news."

As they talked, the waitress shared some thoughts on Elvis.

"I've lived in Memphis all my life; I don't know the city without him. If I were you, I would go out to Graceland fans from all over are creating a makeshift memorial at the gates."

Mary told her; I hope to go out there within the hour and maybe you can get some rest as well."

"No time to rest I'm going out to Graceland once I finish up here.".

Waiting for her order, Mary began the age old McGill tradition of people watching. Her grandmother would have been in heaven she loved to watch people and tonight there were plenty to watch. She was still without food when the waitress came back telling her that unfortunately, her order may take a little longer due to the crowds.

Soon Mary noticed two men looking for a place to set. They made a rather odd duo one a skinny white guy with a full mustache and long stringy hair, appearing he had just escaped a disco and his friend resembled a lightweight black fighter supporting a full afro. Both appeared to be in their early twenties; Mary is drawn to the black guy he appeared somewhat reserved but was resting a large silver box on his shoulder. Mary realized it was a jam box, but she had never seen one quite like this one. The box fits nicely on his shoulder as they moved around the grill searching for a seat. Catching the white guy's eye Mary offered up some good old southern hospitality and suggested they join her. With her new-found sense of adventure, it seemed the right thing to do. Mary informed them if interested the other seats at her table were free, and they were welcomed to join her. Both men quickly thanked her, and each claimed a spot at the table.

Mary had learned long ago a question is not a question if you know the answer, but she still asked. Though both men were wearing Elvis T-shirts, it didn't keep her from asking if they were in town for the funeral. In unison, they said "yes." Both men appeared rather disheveled and gave the impression that they had left in a hurry to get to Memphis. Her father would have said those boys look like they are running from the law and he certainly wouldn't have been pleased with her hospitality. The white one spoke first telling her they were in town to pay their respects and say goodbye to the King. His tone was one of reverence sounding much like a fan. Neither fit the profile for what she considered an Elvis fan. But her view of a typical Elvis fan was changing rapidly. People from all over the world, with various nationalities and cultures, were descending on Memphis. Elvis impacted so many that to characterize his fans would be difficult leading to the change in her thinking.

Mary put on her journalist hat and introduced herself telling them she was there to cover the funeral for her newspaper in Ga. She was not sure if it was her southern accent or the fact she was a female, but both gave her their full attention. The white one wondered where in Georgia? Once she told them, Dublin, she realized neither had ever heard of it, both were courteous enough to ask where's Dublin. She said southern Georgia and told them not to worry it's understandable if they hadn't heard of it. They laughed acknowledging their lack of knowledge when it came to the geography of Georgia. The white one saying this is as far south as either of them had ever been. She smiled telling them not to worry we don't bite. The black one looked a bit nervous and said he sure hoped not. Mary then introduced herself. Both men followed the white one was Jerry Biggs, and the back guy introduced himself as Lynn Petty. Mary asked if they would mind telling her why they decided to come to Memphis and any thoughts they may have about Elvis. They were more than willing to share thoughts with Mary.

They immediately began telling their story, stopping only long enough to order food. Like so many others they were, wanting to say goodbye to the King and give thanks to the man who had given them so much pleasure. Jerry's T-shirt had an image of Elvis in his patent white jumpsuit holding a microphone on stage. Jerry told Mary he was a plumber in New York. Mary asked; "state or city." Though they spoke the same languages, there was a definite difference in deliveries. Jerry responded they were from the city. Lynn then introduced himself as the self-proclaimed leader of the NY-based Black Elvis Fan Club. Mary studied him and said that was quite a title. He showed a sincere grin and added besides being head of this prestigious group he worked for the city. Mary thought here were two average guys who heard the news and decided to get on a plane and come to Memphis hoping to be part of the pageantry and say goodbye to the king of rock n roll. Neither one lacked for enthusiasm when it came to talking about Elvis.

Lynn continued holding the jam box propped up on his right shoulder; Mary could make out he was listening to an Elvis song. Of course, it was Elvis who else. Lynn caught her staring at the box, and told her;

"All Elvis all the time, just another way to pay my respects."

Mary said she had never seen a box like that before.

"It's the latest a tape deck radio combination."

The music continued to play as they spoke. Mary was now even more convinced she needed to get beyond her stereotypical image of an Elvis fan. Lynn helped her realize that Elvis had fans in all shades and ages.

Jerry told her he had been a fan of Elvis all his life; his parents introduced him to the music, and the rest is history. Petty said his path was somewhat different he began listening to the king in high school, adding the music spoke to him. Something in Elvis's delivery stirred his soul. Jerry chimed in that was Elvis. Maybe they were not so unique both shared a love for the man, and his music and Mary was certain she would witness this love and respect from the thousands who were in or on their way to Memphis. What surprised Mary was the fact that they were close to her age and yet had such a love for Elvis.

Roger and Wayne found Mary enjoying her burger and began making their way to her table. She told them she just had to get something to eat; she then introduced them to Lynn and Jerry. Now the five of them sat at the table making what Mary thought must have been an interesting sight. A southern girl two New Yorker's one white one black and two men from England. It was a strange collection. It must have been humorous hearing the different accents all speaking the same language.

Roger was also intrigued with Lynn and Jerry and asked if they would like to join them on the ride out to Graceland. Neither hesitated to accept the offer. Jerry answered for both saying that would be great. Mary thought to herself her solo adventure had now grown to five. One car and five people it had the makings of a great story.

Mary would see the sights with four men she had just meet. Rare air for her, she was not one who usually took chances she was taking on a new persona. Maybe it was the death of Elvis knowing if he could die anyone could die, it's important to live your life while you can. She was now with four new friends; all had arrived in Memphis for various reasons, but now together they would share the experience. Mary and Roger were reporting on the funeral, Wayne supplying the photographs and Jerry and Lynn viewing it. But everyone would be living it, promising to make the next few days exciting.

The grills placemats featured a map of Memphis with highlighted points of interest. It was easy to locate Graceland on the map, and it appeared to be a short distance from the hotel. Mary decided to ask for directions just the same, having little confidence in the placemat map. Mary learned that the mat was fairly accurate and she should have little trouble finding Graceland. Brad still working the front desk then told her she should check out the clubs on Beal St. once done at Graceland. He added the clubs were open late, and there is plenty of fun to be found. Mary thanked him and returned to join the others.

Before they could get out of the grill, a waitress approached Jerry; she was caring a single white daisy, looking older than her probable age. Mary felt this lady resemble what she believed was a stereotypical Elvis fan. Mary felt she was a little less sophisticated and a lot more southern. She realized this was unfair and needed to change her attitude. The Waitress asked if Jerry was going to Graceland. Jerry was a gentleman telling her he was and added he felt it was the right thing to do. She handed him the flower and asked if he would place it at the front gate of Graceland. The Daisy came out of an arrangement at the front desk. Jerry told her; it would be his honor. She grinned gave him a big hug and thanked him and told Jerry she wasn't sure she would be able to make it to Graceland but hoped too. The two of them had made a connection. It struck Mary that Elvis once again was bringing people together, this time, it wasn't his music but his death. So many people would share in the funeral. Jerry summed it up best when he said they considered Elvis family, and when a beloved family member dies, you do your best to be at the funeral. You want to show your love and respect, to the deceased as well as the family. Mary agreed with Jerry's analogy; she had witnessed it at the hospital at the airport, and here at the hotel, Elvis's fans did create one big family. She wondered if Elvis ever realized the size of his family. Mary felt she could learn a lot from these four men. Maybe it was just dumb luck, but now they were together. Things were beginning to work out.

GRACELAND

Roger led the four of them to a 1977 maroon Chevy Impala large enough for everybody. As they walked toward the car, Wayne joked about Rogers driving. He told everyone, it was no small miracle that the car was in one piece and good repair. Roger responded saying not to pay Wayne any attention he didn't appreciate skillful driving and then gave the keys to Mary. Mary liked Roger immediately there was a quality about him that made her feel secure. Jerry, Lynn, and Wayne climbed into the back, and Roger took the passenger side. Jerry sat in the middle so Lynn would have room for his music box. Jerry informed everyone the music box, and Lynn was inseparable to which Lynn offered no argument he did seem rather attached to it.

As Mary started the car Lynn suggested a little music, He turned the volume up on the jam box and appropriately played, *Follow that Dream*. With their musical accompaniment, they pulled out of the parking lot and Mary made a plea for someone to please remember how to get back to the hotel. There was a great deal of traffic considering the time. Everyone must have had the same idea of going to Graceland. As Mary moved into the traffic, to combat her nervousness, she decided to share some of what she had learned about Memphis and its relation to Elvis. She told them how Elvis had purchased Graceland several years ago, but her story was interrupted when everyone noticed a large banner hanging over the street. The banner welcomed the Shriners to Memphis for their 1977 National Convention. Roger was the first to speak saying it appears they would have some company. The National Convention indicated the funeral would not be the only big event taking place in Memphis. Roger asked Mary if she knew anything about the Shriners. Mary then changed the subject from Graceland to the Shriners. She told them;

"the Shriners are a special international fraternal order recognized for their community service."

Roger kiddingly accused her of reading that bit of information right off the banner. Mary smiled but continued talking about the Shriners but wasn't sure anyone cared. The thought of a national convention taking place at such a solemn time appeared to irritate Jerry and Lynn. Though few were interested, Mary's nervous energy propelled her to continue talking. She told them how the Shriners were known for their benevolence in helping cripple children, but they also had quite a reputation for partying. The St. Jude's Children's Hospital in Memphis was one of the largest Shriners hospitals in the world. The Shriners are known for their good work and are said to like to party hardy. At least Roger was listening hearing of the good work and party side of the Shriners' he said that sounded like a nice combination. Mary told them they could recognize the Shriners' by their tassel hats resembling upside-down flower pots. Roger felt Mary knew a lot about the Shriners'. Mary told him;

"the Shriners are very active back in my hometown. It didn't matter 4th of July, Christmas, or Labor Day if you had a parade you could count on seeing the Shriners, driving an assortment of mini cars, motorcycles and some even drove motorized appliances. They are an entertaining group, and should offer up quite a contrast to the funeral goers."

Roger wondered did she say motorized appliances. Laughing Mary replied; "Yea and my favorite was the motorized bathtubs. It made quite a site going down the street followed by a group of mini bikes."

It was a bit surreal thinking there would be a national convention taking place in the city preparing to bury an American legend. Mary felt the Shriners and Elvis at least shared one trait both were known for their generosity as well as their partying spirit. Mary felt the story couldn't get any more intriguing, mourners, Shriners, curiosity seekers, and others would all merge in Memphis. The next few days were going to be eventful.

They had little trouble finding Graceland, only a short drive from the hotel. Once there it was clear they had made the right decision. The crowds indicated Graceland was the place to be. As they drove by the mansion, Jerry commented: "so this is the home of Elvis." Lynn grinned and said, "It appears the man certainly did alright for himself." The crowd was predominately white and middle-aged prompting Lynn to add "I don't believe my group has arrived." Jerry told Lynn;

"Your numbers may be small, but you will be accepted. Elvis was a man of all the people. And besides, with your jam box supplying the sounds, you will be a walking tribute to the King."

The grounds were impressive, but Mary thought was it all seemed a little ornate for her taste. She hoped to get a glimpse of the inside if they did hold a public viewing. The crowds were continuing to grow. The late hour was keeping no one away. Everyone in the car was excited and ready for Mary to find a parking space. Jerry and Lynn were anxious to be with the fans some of which held candles others carried signs, but all had heavy hearts.

They found parking in a neighboring lot the owner was sitting out in a lawn chair holding a flag waving at potential customers. The homemade sign lying next to his chair said parking $2.00. It certainly was a reasonable price considering the demand? But to Mary, it was an illustration of people cashing in on the death of Elvis. A couple of souvenir stands had opened and were selling photo's posters and signs anything they could sell to mark the occasion. Where they parked left them with a decent walk in the warm and muggy night; Mary felt this was a precursor for more hot days.

Once out of the car Jerry and Lynn walked ahead with a fast pace anxious to join the crowds. Jerry was true to his word he had protected the flower given him by the waitress and placing it on the makeshift memorial would be his first stop. A wide arrangement of flowers had already arrived and laid at the entrance. The flowers were a symbol of the love and sorrows so many were feeling. Mary kept her eye on Jerry and Lynn knowing that of the five; they were true fans, and she wanted to see how they reacted. After placing the flower at the gate, Jerry went to join those holding candles with Lynn following.

To the surprise of no one, many of the mourners were still shedding tears. The death had exposed raw emotions. Roger had an interesting thought on the tears telling Mary that they may have been the result of so many people coming together and their sadness playing off one another. As Mary walked toward the main gate, she knew the question of the day was; "Why." Those searching for answers found none. But those hurting found love and support all sharing their feelings for the man and his music. Jerry accepted a candle from a lady; standing in silence, the light from the candle reflected the emotions on his face. Graceland would serve as the epicenter for the story.

With all the sorrow present. Mary was bothered by her excitement for the assignment. Wayne went off to search out potential photo locations he would shoot during the light of day. Mary felt there was no better time to begin her quest for the story within the story; she hoped her excitement could be harnessed not wishing to appear disrespectful.

Mary was looking for some direction and asked Roger where should they start. Roger suggested finding someone who may have information on scheduled events. They spoke to one of the many policemen stationed around the grounds a member of the Memphis Police Department. They found him to be friendly as well as informative. The officer an older gentleman's whose name tag read Crowder. Officer Crowder was polite but not impressed that they were with the press. But fortunately, he did take the time to talk with them. Mary asked Officer Crowder if he knew of anything scheduled regarding the funeral or any other activities for that matter. Crowder said;

"There's plenty of speculation, but as of now, nothing finalized. I feel the family is moving rather quickly to get the funeral scheduled. I did hear the family hoped to move the body back to Graceland later today and then will hold a public viewing."

Much of the info was what she had heard earlier on the TV broadcast, but it was nice to get it from a second source. When Crowder said later today, Mary realized just how late it was getting. Maybe it was the adrenaline rush, but she wasn't feeling tired. Crowder wasn't sure if there would be a separate time for the media to view the body or not but if they do it would be by invitation only. Even if there was a media viewing, Mary knew her chances of being included would be slim unless she could tag along with Roger after all he represented the international press. But she still planned to participate in the public viewing hoping to see the inside of Graceland.

After they had finished speaking with Crowder, Mary took a moment to view the mansion. Many of the rooms showed illumination, and she could only imagine what was taking place behind those walls. Mary wondered how the family would have time to grieve with so much activity inside and outside the mansion. Some movement on the second floor caught her eye. It appeared someone was watching the crowd in a secretive fashion as if they didn't want to be recognized. She wondered who it could be, maybe a family friend or perhaps a celebrity who had come in for the service and was staying at the mansion. She couldn't get a good look at the man as he stayed behind the curtain but whoever it may have been was intently studying the crowd. Mary wondered what the man must he be thinking gazing on the large collection of people milling around the home? She asked Roger to look up at the window and tell her what he thought. Roger said it was probably a bedroom and from the looks of things it appeared someone was keeping tabs on the activity. Adding, he wasn't sure that was the story she was looking for unless it proved to be Elvis rising from the grave. Roger felt it could be anybody a heavy-set male, who didn't want to be seen or recognized.

Mary said, "It's just a bit eerie how he keeps looking over the crowd as if he is looking for someone or something."

Roger laughed telling her; "You have the makings of a great journalist with your wondering mind; I hadn't even noticed the man."

Mary thought how strange it must be staying in the house with so many people milling around on the outside causing enough commotion to raise the dead if not Elvis himself.

After about an hour, Roger and Wayne were ready to leave. Though

Mary had spoken with a few mourners they were not as receptive as she had hoped, maybe it was the late hour or the darkness of the night. She felt she would have more luck during the day; sunshine tends to open people up. Roger suggested they find Beale St and experience some of the Memphis music scene and famous nightlife and enjoy a drink before going back. Mary knew she couldn't sleep, so Beale St sounded good. Graceland then Beale Street it looked as if it would be her first all-night adventure in awhile.

Though late, the clubs remained opened as Memphis prepared for thousands of visitors. Unlike Dublin, Memphis would be open well into the morning hours. Mary located Jerry and Lynn and told them of their plans. Neither was keen on leaving; both would have been content to stay at Graceland. They were not that interested in going to a club, but neither was ready to go back to the hotel either. They had heard the rumor about the public viewing and wanted to be there for that. Roger assured them there would amble time for the viewing. Jerry looked to Lynn for guidance both seemed uncertain then Jerry said;

"Maybe a change of venue might do us some good. Who knows maybe you will find more members of that fan club you profess to be president."

Lynn said he was in, but the box was going with him. It seemed a bit strange to Mary, but they were at the funeral of the King and the rules of society were being altered, why not let someone into a club with their music. Mary suggested Lynn insist it was a personal tribute to the king. The five of them once again made their way to the car, another chapter awaited.

Mary was still curious about the man spotted on the second floor. She couldn't help feel it strange that someone would be so secretive keeping watch over the crowd. Pulling out of the parking lot, Mary asked Lynn and Jerry if they noticed the man at the window. Jerry was first to mention he had seen the man but was unable to make anything out other than someone was there and he was a little spooky in how he viewed the crowd. Lynn said a guy near him claimed the man looked like Elvis, but I only saw a shadowy figure. Claiming the man looked like Elvis may have been a bit of wishful thinking. Mary knew the thought of Elvis viewing his memorial now that would be quite a story. Whoever it was sure was secretive. Roger said;

"People will see what they want to see. You can expect all kinds of rumors, but personally, I feel it was a family friend or maybe someone working security at the mansion. Surely we can all agree it wasn't Elvis."

Wayne laughed saying if it was Elvis then that was a photo he needed to get. But if it were Elvis then this trip would be unnecessary. Everyone laugh as they were becoming a little punchy due to the time.

Soon the crowds were gone, and the traffic was diminishing. Graceland was the place to be, but they hoped to discover more. Thus, far Mary had seen the airport the hotel and Graceland it was time for another slice of Memphis. She welcomed the change as they drove toward the river area and Beale Street again following their placemat map.

THE HOUSE OF MUSIC

Though Beale St may be known as the home of the blues, it was clear there were plenty of options when it came to music. Judging from the marquees of several of the clubs, no matter your musical taste it could be satisfied. The late hour did not limit the choices. They decided on a club located on a side street west of Beale appropriately named The House of Music.

The House of Music was in what must have been a large department store in a previous life. The ample parking out front made the decision easy. As the group reached the door, Lynn had no trouble getting into the club with his music box. The young man at the door looked to be a college student and if he had any concerns about Lynn and his box he didn't show it? Mary was thinking the sight of a black man carrying a jam box playing Elvis tunes was not the usual fare for any club. But on this night the unusual was the norm. Everyone felt welcomed, music box and all. The entrance took you through two black swinging doors each with The House of Music painted above a window in the upper half of the door. The widow gave a porthole view of a large room featuring a bar and dance floor. The club was probably busier than usual, especially for a Tuesday night. A strange mix made up the crowd it was hard to tell if they were mourners, Shriners, or locals.

It took a while for their eyes to adjust to the dimly lit club. The room could have easily been someone's basement just on a much grander scale. The walls decorated with posters and photographs of musical artist. Take away the large bar and dance floor, and you could have been in a dorm room at UGA. A parquet dance floor occupied the middle of the room surrounded by tables and chairs that appeared to be flowing onto the dance floor. The outer sections of the room featured large overstuffed sofas. In keeping with the basement theme, there was a large display of stereo components serving as decorations, a few of the tables looked like large speakers. A DJ in the corner supplied the music, and once he noticed their group he gave out a house of music welcome, he welcomed everyone who came through the swinging doors. He was a high-energy DJ promoting drinks music and dance not necessarily in that order.

The five of them found a table to the right of the dance floor. When the waitress came to the table, you could sense she was fascinated with Lynn and his Jam Box. She recognized the music coming out of the box and immediately inquired about Lynn's favorite Elvis songs. She leaned down to get a listen, and the two of them seemed removed from everyone else as they listen to the song *Moody Woman*. Lynn, the self-proclaimed leader of the black Elvis fan club, was increasing the membership one song at a time. Soon he told her he was a big fan of the early hits. When *Moody Woman* finished *Are, You Lonesome Tonight* started up. She immediately said oh I love that one and Lynn said she wasn't alone and it was one of his personal favorites. Lynn demonstrated he knew the music, as well as liked it. Mary was beginning to appreciate the depth of Lynn and Jerry's Elvis knowledge. While the song played, Jerry leaned over and joined Lynn in singing the chorus. The waitress was all smiles. She finally took their orders telling Jerry and Lynn she would be back for more tunes. Mary decided to be alcohol-free for the remainder of the night and ordered a ginger ale. Not only was she doing the driving but with so much going on she wanted to embrace it all, and her tolerance for alcohol was not her best trait. Lynn and Jerry asked for a Budweiser's staying close to their English roots Roger and Wayne order up scotches. They were soon talking about the club and the energetic DJ. The sound coming out of the DJ booth was a pleasant alternative to the Elvis music.

After she had gotten her drink, Mary decided to venture into the unknown and do a little investigative work. Leaving the table, Mary heard Roger announced he was going to meet some of the local talents, to which Wayne told him to be careful reminding him it is an emotional night. The local talent he was speaking of happened to be a group ladies gathered near the bar. His freestyle and cool mannerism were sure to impress, add his English accent, and there may indeed be a need to be careful.

Mary went straight to the bar she had learned early in her college life if you ever needed to know what was going on at the club always check with those working the bar. You can gather a lot of information from a bartender, and they know the locals better than anyone. On her short walk to the bar, Mary could hear others talking about Elvis and his death; the story was now replaying over and over.

A group of Shriners recognizable by their hats surrounded the DJ booth making a request. Mary heard one say "see if he's got *The Streak*." She thought that's all they needed was a revival of the streak. Though there were many conversations about Elvis, his death did not deter some from taking to the dance floor. An army clad in polyester moved freely with the beat of the music. Disco was alive and well at The House of Music.

She approached a bartender who looked to be close to her age and once she caught his attention he moved her way. Mary leaned over introduced herself telling him she was a reporter for a paper in Georgia and was hoping to get a story about Elvis something a little different from the usual. Trying to be heard over the crowd and the music he surprisingly told Mary she was his first reporter. She explained her desire to get a feel for how the public is reacting to the death. He smiled and told her;

"You've come to the right place we are busier than usual. For most, I feel the news is just sinking in, so you will find some who feel the news is a cruel joke other's claiming the mob killed him. You name it; everyone has a theory. There will be plenty to write Elvis's was the king of rock n roll, and Memphis was his home, so you'll find folks questioning and analyzing everything."

He recommended she stay away from the Shriners they seem oblivious to it all. They were there to have a good time and had been partying since they arrived. He then pulled out a Shriner's hat from under the bar saying it was awarded to him last night for being the fastest bartender in the tri-state region per the great potentate Robert Bridges. Mary just smiled.

The bartender suggested she talk to a gentleman standing at the far end of the bar. The man was heavy-set, wearing a gray cowboy hat and a maroon sports coat. He had been telling stories all night. Mary figured she could buy him a drink and get a story a small price to pay. The bartender suggested she ask him about his uncle and the Cadillac. Adding he couldn't guarantee any truth to the story, but it was a story she should hear. Mary asked what he was drinking and proceeded to order up a Blue Ribbon for the man in the gray cowboy hat. The beer hopefully would be her ticket to hearing the story.

As Mary got closer to the man, she noticed his faded jeans and maroon jacket clashed with his oversized cowboy hat. Judging from his appearance, she should be in for quite an interview. It looked as if he was holding court with a small group telling a story about a time he saw Elvis at a hardware store. She waited for a break in his story before making eye contact and offering him the beer. As he grinned and enjoyed his fifteen minutes of fame, she told him she understood PBR was his drink of choice and she was hoping to talk with him about Elvis. He took the beer and said; "that's a first, a pretty lady buying me a beer." Mary introduced herself telling him she was a reporter from a paper in Georgia and she understood he had a few stories to share about Elvis. Taking the beer, he said thank you and then added he loved talking about the King and asked what she would like to know. Mary could tell he was impressed by her youth and looks, so he gave her his full attention. Mary said;

"I was hoping to get a fan's perspective something you feel would be important for others to learn about Elvis."

He smiled and said, "Well pretty lady I will be happy to help you out."

"Maybe you could tell me about your uncle and a Cadillac. I understand that's a good one."

"Oh, yea that is a good one."

It was evident he had been drinking for a while as he introduced himself as Tim Brown and told Mary he had lived in Memphis his entire life and been an Elvis fan just as long. Mary gave him a flirtatious smile and asked him to tell her about his uncle and the Cadillac. "That's a good one. You'll find it interesting it shows you the kind of man Elvis was." His drunken behavior did not prevent him from being polite, and she was again thanked for the beer and then gave Mary his full attention. He didn't seem to care that she represented a small-town paper he was flattered that the press wanted to talk with him.

Tim told Mary that many had heard it, but it was still a good story. Taking a long drink from the beer Brown began to talk:

"It was back in the spring of 1960 just after Elvis received his discharge from the Army. I guess you knew Elvis was in the army."

Mary nodded, and he continued.

"Even in the Army Elvis never lost contact with his fans. He may have been away for a couple of years, but his music remained popular and we the fans remained loyal. Anyone discharged from the Army can tell you it's happy time I know it was for me but that's a different story, and you wanted to hear about Elvis."

Mary thought that if she ever did hear the story, it better be good considering the time he was taking.

"Well, Elvis was no exception when he got his discharge he was a happy man. And receiving an honorable discharge meant a great deal to him, and he would finally be able to return to his family and career. Everyone coming out of the Army gets a separation check. The check is supposed to make the transition from Army life to civilian life a little easier."

Tim began to laugh telling her Elvis's separation check was for 106 dollars.

"Can you imagine Elvis being excited over 106 dollars he used to make a hundred times that in one show. But Elvis was regular Army, and he had 106 dollars coming to him. I'd compare giving Elvis such a small amount was like giving the Mississippi a cup of water."

Brown began to repeat himself, "It was the spring of 1960. Elvis received his honorable discharge and returned to Memphis." Mary encouraged him to get back to the story. Returning to the story, Brown told her;

"Elvis had been in the Army for two years, and he needed a new car. And Elvis was a Cadillac man; when it came to cars, the man loved his Cadies. Elvis like anyone was excited about his honorable discharge and evidently, it put him in a giving mood."

Brown took another swallow of his beer and laughed;

"Yea he was going to share the wealth. Elvis was always generous, a trait that made many love him. As it happened, my uncle, Jim was in the right place at the right time. Jim was working at Wonder Cadillac and was lucky enough to be there the day Elvis and his father Vernon came shopping for a new Cadillac."

Mary learned Browns Uncle Jim had only been working at Wonder for a short while trying his hand at selling cars. Brown described his Uncle as a people person someone who loved to be in the middle of everything and selling cars seemed to be a good fit. He went on to say;

"Jim had always enjoyed Elvis's music, but the day he walked into Wonder Cadillac Jim became a lifetime fan as did some others. It was quite a day Elvis had come to buy a new car, and before he left Wonder Cadillac, he had purchased seven and gave five away. The funny thing is he didn't even drive the cars before giving them away? Let's see Jim got one Ray Sellers in sales got one, Bob Boswell in parts and Rhonda White the receptionist each got one, and one of the mechanics got another and Elvis, and his Daddy took the other two. Jim loved to tell how Elvis told everyone he could afford the cars after all the government had given him a $106.00. Damn that's funny Elvis was quite a jokester, and he sure made five people happy that day. That small check motivated Elvis and his giving spirit. He spent close to 20,000 dollars that day. Not only did Elvis loved Cadillac's he loved sharing his wealth as well."

Brown took another drink from his beer and looked at Mary and told her with a reflective smile,

"Elvis gave many a car away it just wasn't that day he just liked doing it. My Uncle Jim kept that car for nearly ten years, drove it till it wouldn't drive anymore. He just didn't want to get rid of it. And, who could blame him it was a gift from Elvis, and that's pretty damn special."

Brown finished the beer and Mary sensed he wouldn't mind if is she bought him another. She motioned to the bartender for another ginger as well as another PBR for her friend. After ordering the drinks, she asked if he would get back to Elvis. He smiled and thanked her for the beer and then said;

"Elvis loved cars, and as a poor kid, he would often fantasize about fancy cars but especially the Cadillac. Elvis felt the Cadillac was a symbol of success."

Brown then got a little more serious, and somewhat philosophical maybe it was the beer talking, but Brown said he felt when Elvis was giving and helping others he didn't have to look at his life.

"I'm no doctor, but it seems to me Elvis felt better when he was sharing his wealth." Mary smiled saying; "You know what they say it's better to give than receive but it appears Elvis did plenty of both." Brown acknowledged this was true of Elvis. He never felt Elvis was ever truly comfortable with his wealth or fame. He felt this may have been a result of his upbringing, coming from such an impoverished home.

Mary tried to get Brown back on the subject, of his uncle and the Caddy. Brown apologized telling her he gets carried away when he talks about Elvis. Once again, she asked about the Caddy and his uncle. He then said;

"there was not much more to tell Jim said he learned Elvis had made nearly $125,000 when he appeared on the Frank Sinatra show making the expense of the cars manageable."

Mary jotted down the info about the Sinatra show she didn't realize Sinatra had a variety show until Brown mentioned it. Brown went on saying if he made that kind of money for one show he could afford the cars. Brown was feeling the effects of his many beers as he once again started talking about Elvis's wealth and how he liked to share it with others. Mary knew she would get little more from him and thanked him for his time and the story. He told her anytime and then gave her his name once again and his address. She took down his name address and thanked him. As she was excusing herself Brown wanted to add something else making it apparent the alcohol was beginning to talk he said;

"Listen you can believe what you want, but you should know Elvis was a good man and he did a lot of good for the common man. You should focus on the good, not the bad no drugs no violence."

She assured him she wasn't interested covering the negative. Others could report on the rumors; she would try to convey the outpouring of love so evident by the thousands who have come to Memphis for the funeral. Mary said she would do her best to honor the memory of Elvis. As Mary turned to walk away, she heard Brown tell a woman standing near him that he was helping the local press learn more about Elvis. He enjoyed being the center of attention.

As Mary walked back to the table, she noticed Roger had the full attention of a lady who must have been falling for his English charm. The lady looked as if she had lived a country song and the lyrics rode hard and put up wet could have easily applied. Dressed in a tight-fitting blue dress, she was revealing enough cleavage to gain any man's attention. With a drink in one hand and a cigarette in another Mary got the impression she would like to give Roger more than her attention. When Mary caught Roger's eye, he smiled and announced Dublin Scribe had returned. Mary laughed and asked if she could join them. Roger's newest friend wasn't overly thrilled with the proposition. She wanted Roger all to herself. But before she could protest Roger told her Mary was with their party and she was covering the funeral for her paper in Georgia. Mary sensed the lady was not interested in talking, viewing Mary as competition for Roger's attention. The lady asked Mary if she had been talking to Tim Brown. Evidently, she had noticed her earlier. "Yes, he's quite interesting." The lady said interesting is not the word she would use and told Mary to be careful Brown's known to spin a tale or two. She then added she was sure he was flattered to have a pretty, young reporter giving him attention. The young reporter commit seemed to be more a putdown than a compliment. But Mary let it go and told her thanks for the heads up. Roger may have sensed the lady's frustration, so he tried to bring Mary into their conversation. He introduced Mary to the lady saying Kathy here has an interesting story she knew Elvis personally, and she was just about to give some insight into Elvis's younger years. He then said;

"Kathy worked in the studio where Elvis began his recording career." Mary let Kathy know she was impressed. Then Roger added; "pretty exciting huh?"

With that statement and Rogers charm, Kathy brightens up once she realized she would remain the main attraction. After all, she was the one who knew Elvis, and she would still have Rogers attention. Mary looked at her "So you knew Elvis." Kathy responded;

"Oh, honey I knew him all right. Tim didn't tell you he knew him did he"?

Mary assured her he had not Mary told her Brown had shared a story of his uncle Jim and the gift of a Cadillac. Kathy smiled and said;

"Tim loves to tell that story who knows if it's true."

Mary found Tim's story interesting but it was second hand, this lady could give a first-person account. Firsthand knowledge was always better than stories. Mary was guilty of being impressed with someone for just knowing Elvis. Mary questioned Kathy saying you worked in the recording business and that was all the lead she needed.

Kathy took a sip from her glass and began telling them how she worked for Sun Records and Sam Phillips back in the fifties. She was rather condescending saying I'm sure you've heard of them. Maybe Roger felt the need to run a little interference because he looked at her smiled and replied they were very much aware of Sam Phillips and his work. The truth was Mary had little knowledge of Phillips only learning about his connection with Elvis from Alan Conrad on the flight to Memphis. Roger said he understood that Phillips was instrumental in launching quite a few careers including Elvis. Kathy then said;

"I knew them all Conway Twitty, Johnny Cash, BB King, Roy Orbison and Jerry Lee, all superstars, but Elvis was the biggest."

Trying to remain in the conversation Mary told Kathy;

"Wow, you worked with some of the greats."

Kathy then told them;

"I loved working for Sam. In the beginning, it was just fun hanging out with the guys little did I know how big they would become they were far from household names when I knew them. It was an exciting and invigorating time for sure, for many of the guys the studio was a home away from home. They would come and just hang out playing and dreaming. Phillips was a smart man he recognized each artist had their emerging style and energy, and he wanted to harness that energy and make them successful. The energy in the place was something, and the talent was just wonderful."

She may have continued to babble about the studio. But Roger brought her back to Elvis saying; "I would love to hear some of the stories about Elvis."

Not deterred Kathy kept telling them about Sam Phillips and the studio. They soon learned from Kathy that Phillips had chosen the name Sun Records to emphasize the positive feelings one gets from the Sun bright warm inviting. Saying; "That was Sam's vision, always saying there was nothing more positive than a new day and beautiful sunrise, he was an eternal optimist." Kathy soon returned to Elvis telling them he wasn't much different from the others maybe a little politer and rather shy but he was comfortable at the studio. She told them;

"Elvis seemed to gain self-confidence when he sang it was as if the music gave him permission to be someone else. He was young when Sam discovered him. It was more luck than discovery, lucky for Sam. Elvis stumbled into the studio and helped make Sun Records a part of Rock N Roll history."

Roger asked what, she thought made Sam so interested in Elvis. Kathy told them;

"That was easy it was his sound Sam had been looking for a special sound he wanted a white guy that sounded black. Not only did Elvis have the sound but he also had the energy. His energy and sound would appeal to thousands. Sam's dream was to find an artist that could appeal to both audiences black and white and Elvis was that man. Before Elvis came to the studio, Sam would often say; if he could find someone to appeal to blacks and whites, the results would be solid gold. I guess he was right. Sam and Elvis both benefited from each other Sam launched Elvis's career, and Elvis helped launch Sun Records."

Mary began to make some notes looking for a way to soften

Kathy's disdain she asked if she would mind if she quoted her and used her name. Kathy responded;

"Sure, honey it's Kathy Morgan."

One thing Mary learned in college, most people, loved to see their name in print and Kathy was no exception. She continued with her story telling them that she began working for Sun Records only a month after the studio opened. Kathy looking at Mary said;

"I was about your age when I started. I'd come in after secretarial school to work. At first, I answered the phone and did odd jobs everything from filing to cleaning up. But once I finished school I began working full time and stayed with Sam for many years. When I met Elvis, he was a shy boy who drove a delivery truck for a living. There was something about him that drew you toward him, more than his good looks he had a presence and that presence shined through even though he was very shy. I knew he was special the first day I laid eyes on him. It was more than a school girls crush. He was so polite referring to everyone as Sir and Maim no matter their age or race he was just a good person. One thing you can quote me on Elvis had a heart of gold. He always took the time to say hello. The only reason he even came into the studio was to record a record for his Mama. Just think if he hadn't wanted to do something special for her we might not be here today. Thank God he loved his mother."

She then turned emotional telling them the world would be better off if everyone loved their Mama like Elvis did. Kathy was a fan, but she did make a good point about luck. It seems success is often a combination of luck and timing. From her story, Mary assumed Kathy was in her 40's maybe not as old as she looked. Mary also felt, Kathy's story much like Browns may have been embellished a little by the alcohol.

Tonight, everyone had an Elvis story so why not listen. Kathy continued to talk; telling them;

"Elvis would come to the recording studio and spend hours strumming his guitar trying to master a sound. Kathy told them Elvis was a gentleman not like so many of the others. Elvis would come to the studio and spend hours strumming his guitar trying to master a sound. He was a gentleman. Those other guys thought their music gave them permission for casual sex none of them wanting a relationship just looking to screw. Heaven forbids any of them ever sell a record that just made them feel they were entitled to sex."

Mary felt Kathy was trying to give Roger a clue with the sex talk, indicating if he was interested she was available. Mary wasn't sure if Roger was going to bite after all he seemed to be the perfect gentleman. But maybe Mary was reading too much into Kathy's non-verbals. Roger's then surprised Mary when he said to Kathy; "It sounds like you may have been the target of some of the musicians."

Grinning Kathy answers; "You can say that not all those boys were gentlemen. It was a wild time young and impulsive."

Roger gave her his best James Bonn look and asked did she ever sleep with Elvis? Kathy was far less surprised by the question than Mary after hearing his question she just smiled reached across the table took Rogers hand and said;

"Honey, you should know a southern lady never tells of her conquest. But if I had I'm sure it would have been great. Elvis would put you first just like he did his fans and family. If you weren't happy, he would worry. Like I said he was shy and only when he was playing his music did he seem comfortable with others."

Mary was beginning to feel a little uncomfortable with Kathy's efforts to seduce Roger so she told them she needed another drink and asked if she could bring them anything. Mary felt if Roger wanted a chance to experience some of what Ms. Morgan had learned, he would not have asked for another drink, and she would have stayed away. Kathy immediately said no she was fine but Roger sensing an opportunity to exit the conversation said he needed another scotch. Roger took Kathy's hand said he hoped she would excuse him and added it had been a real pleasure. Mary sensed Kathy's disappointment this exit did not appear to be what she had desired.

Kathy said the pleasure was mutual. Telling them, she should get back to her table, but if Roger needed anything else she would be there for a while, she then gave him a hug thrusting her breast on him and said you just let me know. Kathy then wrote her phone number down on a napkin and handed it to him. If her hug wasn't enough of an invitation, she leaned over and gave him a kiss on the check and said I hope to see you later. Mary told her it was nice to meet her though she wasn't sure Kathy even heard her. After Kathy had left the table Mary smiled at Roger and mocked Kathy statement;

"Honey if you need anything and I mean anything just give me a call."

Roger looked at her and with a wicked grin saying "Kathy seemed like a rather nice lady wouldn't you say." Mary laughed and said oh yes rather nice indeed. She then wondered if Roger would need anything from Kathy. He began to laugh and saying he hoped not.

The bartender greeted Roger and Mary on their return to the bar. He asked Mary how her interview with Tim went. Mary told him;

"Interesting but I found Kathy Morgan to be a piece of work. According to Kathy, I should be careful about what to believe when it comes to Tim."

The bartender told Mary that Kathy and Tim were both regulars and their paths crossed often. He then asked what he could get for them. Mary said she was staying with ginger ale and Roger settle for another Johnny Walker and a hint of water.

Returning to the table Roger and Mary passed Kathy's table, and she made a point to make eye contact and smile. You had to give her credit she was persistent. With Kathy, no longer with them, Mary shared the Tim Brown story about his uncle. Telling Roger, it certainly had been an informative night, and it seems Elvis was very generous and had plenty of fans who will always speak of his kindness. Roger added Elvis was an interesting figure and in death, that interest has just intensified. He left behind thousands of fans all with stories to tell.

It was a night full of positive reflections of Elvis. No one dare speak ill of the man. Tonight, the conversation was limited to the memories of a country boy from Tupelo Mississippi who rose to be a star in Memphis and the world.

Mary and Roger continued to talk about what they had learned. Soon Wayne came to the table and told them he had met a man who was quite interesting. Wayne told them the man seemed to believe the death may not be real but rather a hoax of some kind. The statement surprised both causing them to begin questioning Wayne. Wayne pulled out a chair and began telling them about the gentleman he met earlier. He had met a private investigator who claimed his work as a PI has led him to a rather interesting and a tad disturbing story.

Wayne told them the private investigator had some suspensions surrounding the death and went as far to say it could all be an elaborate hoax. Roger thought Wayne was kidding. He questioned how and why. Mary chimed in saying the bartender did say a few felt the news was a cruel joke. Roger shook his head; telling them,

"Unbelievable but when you cover enough of these events, you can count on a few nuts coming out of the woodwork. These nuts will speculate on everything; nothing should come as a surprise, but this one takes the cake."

Wayne said, "well this nut happens to be a private investigator with a few credentials."

Mary reminded them that there were plenty in denial, but she felt this was more a result of grief. Wayne continued telling them they may just want to hear the investigator out it's probably just a theory, but it's an interesting one. As Roger took another drink, he said: "not dead now that would be a story." Mary shook her head saying;

"they always told us to have an open mind when following a story but this maybe a little much. It seems crazy considering the news reports."

Wayne acknowledged it might be crazy but felt they should hear the PI out. He told them he didn't talk long with the PI but in the short conversation, he learned a lot, he felt Elvis was looking for some relief and faking his death may have been just the ticket. Roger stated; "death gives you get permanent relief a big difference from just canceling a tour."

Wayne told them;

"The P-I believes Elvis may have been looking for a permanent solution to all the demands and death was indeed a permanent solution. This guy says that Elvis was being swallowed up by his life and his celebrity status, he was desperate for a way out."

Mary felt he was making a good case for suicide, not a hoax. Who knows the P I felt Elvis was trying to get away from the spotlight and out of public scrutiny? Roger being the devil's advocate says to Wayne;

"So, this P I feels a man who enjoyed the lifestyle of a king and was adored by thousands would stage his death to get away from it all,"

"I know it's crazy and far-fetched, but the guy seemed rational, and something about him and his theories made me think it may be worth hearing."

Mary knew from her time in J-school one should hear the story before making any assumptions, but she found this theory hard to accept. Wayne told them he had invited the P-I over to talk. Mary felt even if it's just a theory it something she should hear. Everyone agreed it would be hard to believe, but it couldn't hurt to hear the man out. Mary saw it as a headline one would see on a supermarket tabloid, not the Dublin Journal. But who could resist hearing such a tale?

Jerry and Lynn were in an upbeat mood both welcomed throughout the club thanks to Lynn's walking tribute to Elvis. With the jam box and a large collection of tapes, they were opening doors of acceptance making friends wherever they went. Neither was having trouble fitting in.

Mary began telling Lynn and Jerry about her interview with Brown and the free Cadillac when a tall, slender man walked over to the table; Wayne rose from his chair and introduced the gentleman as Matt Saunders, the Private Investigator he had met.

Mary felt he resembled a conservatively dressed accountant more than a P I. Wayne thanked him for stopping by and then introduced everyone. After introductions, Mary asked his specialty. Saunders said he did basic P I work; insurance fraud, cheating husbands various stuff; He told her he had been working the Memphis area for over twenty years. Quoting a song from Elvis, he told them he helped those with Suspicious Minds. Jerry and Lynn were immediately impressed with his reference to one of their favorite tunes. Saunders said he had done his share of work with the entertainment industry primarily over copyright infringements and contract disputes. Adding he worked for some producers wanting to learn more about their client's everything from drug use to womanizing.

Roger moved quickly to the point, telling Saunders that "Wayne said you might have some questions about Elvis's death."

Saunders simply replied;

"You could say that. The nature of my business causes one to question everything, and Elvis's death is no exception. Let me put it this way there's room for some healthy speculation based on life as a private eye and my years of following Elvis. The work I've done for the music industry has given me a different perspective on its stars. I know how crazy it sounds but before anyone ask no I'm not one of those fans who refuses to believe Elvis could die. Though I've never had a case involving Elvis I've learned a lot about Memphis's number one talent through my work. I considered it an occupational hazard, but over the years I've developed a skeptical mind. I figured there might be more to the death or non-death than is being reported. First, consider the circumstances of the death no one's getting the whole story."

Mary reminded Saunders that death comes in many forms even for those rich and famous. Saunders acknowledged he was making quite a jump from thinking there should be more information about the death to thinking the whole story could be made up. Mary couldn't imagine someone of Elvis's stature wanting to fake his death and even if he did pulling off such a scheme seemed almost impossible. Saunders asked them to consider it this way; if people felt it was impossible wouldn't it be easier to do it. Roger felt Saunders was talking in circles and asked what he was trying to say. Saunders stated that if something is considered impossible, then few would consider the possibility of it to happen. Mary thought he was making little sense. Saunders then asked everyone to keep an open mind reminding them that there is always more to the story. He then added to pull off such a charade it would take someone with Elvis's status and resources. Wayne joined in and said the man certainly had the resources.

Saunders smiled and said;

"While the world mourned his death, Elvis could escape no longer living in the public limelight. Elvis's fans would be too upset for any questions."

Mary skeptically asked;

"Why on earth would he want to fake his death? He had the lifestyle of a king,"

"That's just it the average Joe had no idea what type of life Elvis was living. In the last few years, Elvis has been fighting his share of demons."

Roger wondered "what demons?" Saunders said daemons like drug addiction, increased depression and insecure feelings some would say he was in free fall, a fall he just couldn't stop. Saunders went on to say; "I feel people close to Elvis were manipulating him and he couldn't tell his friends from his enemies; you could say he was drowning and couldn't find a life preserver, the pressure was taking its toll."

Roger then said that all might be true, but it hardly gives credence to one faking their death that's a hard theory to accept. Saunders smiled and said;

"That's why it's a brilliant plan no one would believe it. Think about it if Elvis felt he needed a change something much greater than canceling a tour, it would require a changed mindset and to fake one's death would be the ultimate ticket for change. No more public appearances, no more pressure he could finally find peace. Elvis had the money what he wanted was his freedom. Pulling off such a charade may have been the only way Elvis saw out."

Mary questioned;

"Couldn't he just retire people retire all the time Frank Sinatra did it several times and when he tired of retirement he came back to work you see it every day, retiring from the limelight has got to be easier than faking one's death,"

"I'm not sure anyone would have believed he was retired; the public wouldn't accept it, and then you include the hanger owners who looked to Elvis as their personal money machine they would have continually pressured him to return to the stage. I don't think Elvis could handle retirement any better than he was handling being a celebrity. Fans can be greedy and demanding pulling him out of retirement."

Saunders didn't feel Elvis saw retirement as an option. Elvis needed something more substantial, and death is as substantial, as it gets. Mary said, "it still sounded like an argument for suicide." Saunders said;

"I know it's difficult to believe such a theory, but I don't feel Elvis would have ever considered suicide, because of how his fans would have responded he cared so much for them. It might be crazy thinking, but I believe Elvis might have thought a public death would be more accepting after all death by natural causes is hard to question."

Roger agreed;

"No one can blame you for dying, but if you take your life, then there will be plenty of blame."

Saunders agreed suicide would have affected Elvis's legacy and possibly his estate's future earnings. Mary wasn't buying any of it. How could one choose to fabricate such an illusion and how would it ever be successful? Not to mention the number of people needed to pull it off. Mary agreed it made for a heck of a story just not a believable one. Saunders assured her if Elvis did fake his death only a few of his closest friends would know the truth. Leaving everyone else to mourn along with the rest of the world.

Mary again questioned why. Saunders then said;

"Elvis had difficulty telling others no. He had a need to please not disappoint, this difficulty in telling others no was a contributor to many of his problems and it's hard to ask a dead man for favors."

Mary repeated the notion to Saunders; "So you believe Elvis may have orchestrated a death hoax in hopes of gaining control over his life.

"I couldn't phrase it any better myself."

Roger and Mary both asked what he meant by gaining control over his life. Saunders laughing said;

"I take it neither of you was a traditional Elvis fans, or you would know the last several years, Elvis's life has been anything but normal if anything it's been a hell of a roller coaster ride. A coaster has high points and low points throughout the ride, and lately, that's how Elvis's career has gone. Even his health was questionable with excessive weight gains and alleged drug use his life was becoming uncontrollable, a hell on earth. Though he had thousands of fans, he was a man who felt lost and alone, quite a burden for such a giver. Of course, this is just speculation not sure you could find much support for my theory. But the stories circulating, are just nagging at me. My gut tells me there is more to it, and I refused to believe Elvis died of natural causes. Hell, he was only 42, he may not have been the picture of health but natural causes at 42 come on. If he is dead, you can bet there were some unnatural causes that led up to it".

Mary said she understood his feeling about the natural causes but said it was quite a leap to assume it's a hoax. Saunders agreed it's an occupational hazard.

Saunders became solemn telling them he felt Elvis's decline could be traced back to his divorce from Priscilla reminding everyone Priscilla was Elvis's first love and some would say his only love. He continued;

"They were quite young when they met. Both seemed to bear some responsibility for the divorce. I've investigated enough cheating spouses to tell you it's hard to forgive and forget. Making it almost impossible for love to survive. When they split Elvis's, life seemed to spiral downhill with his womanizing and drug use trying to escape the life he was living. His drug use led to a hospitalization back in 73. I believe it was barbiturates. If he is dead, then I would put my money on the drugs being a contributor. But I just can't shake this notion of a hoax."

Saunders wasn't interested in what may have killed Elvis but choose to look at why he may still be alive. He also told the group that not only was Elvis's personal life going downhill his career and his finances were both taking on water; Saunders felt Elvis couldn't see any way out of the rut. Mary began questioning Saunders;

"If Elvis was in such a funk how could he pull off such an elaborate scheme, I still think suicide would be more likely,"

Saunders said; I just can't see Elvis exiting that way; maybe it was the fan in me. Some would say his lifestyle was a slow suicide anyway. For argument, sake considers the possibility of it being a hoax. Such a scheme would provide a perfect platform for Elvis to find solitude. Saunders reminded them if you are dead, its' hard for others to make demands on you. You can't get blood from a turnip as they say and getting money from a dead man may be just as hard. The man had made some bad investment causing quite a few financial losses contributing to his need to tour. His life was in a real catch 22 he needed a break from touring, but he needed to tour to support his lifestyle."

Mary wondered if the weight problems Saunders spoke of were something he felt bothered Elvis. Saunders said;

"How could he not have been bothered he was becoming a caricature of himself a subject of ridicule for comedians and the tabloids? Even though he was only in his forties career wise, he was old, and I feel he desired to be the young, vibrant, Elvis Presley, again."

Roger returned to the first question wanting to know why Saunders believe Elvis could still be alive. Saunders backtracked a little saying he wasn't sure what to think but felt there was much more to the story than was being told. He knew it sounded crazy but felt it was something to considered;"

Elvis needed to be loved, and the love he knew was disappearing first it was Pricilla, and lately, he feared he was losing fans."

Saunders then asked if they were aware of the book Elvis's close friends and former bodyguards had just published a very critical book on his life. Mary spoke first saying she had not heard that before. Saunders said;

"Not sure of the title something like *Elvis: What Happened?* It hasn't been out long, most likely a money grab by these so-called friends. But they claim it was written to get Elvis to look at his behavior and hopefully prevent him from destroying himself. I haven't read it, but supposedly it was very embarrassing and detrimental adding not the image Elvis wanted his fans to see. Though their tactics were questionable, it does give a little credence to all the rumors and stories floating around about Elvis battling depression and drug abuse."

Mary was tired of the subject, after all, it was just speculation with limited substance so she asks if she could change the conversation. Mary asked Saunders want they should expect over the next couple of days. Saunders said;

"I'm afraid it's going to be a zoo around here the mayor has already canceled all leaves for the police, and President Carter has sent in the National Guard to help with security. People from all over the world will be coming in making the next few days challenging. And that's the sad part; I don't feel Elvis understood the love his fans had for him. Maybe this was a result of his upbringing his family was poor, and once he made it, he felt the need to continue proving he had made it never really enjoying his success always looking for approval."

Mary told Saunders he sounded more like a psychologist rather than a PI. Saunders smiled and said it just comes with the job. Mary realized if Elvis was insecure and in need of approval, others could easily take advantage of him and his wealth.

Mary's efforts to change the topic fell on deaf ears as Saunders continued to talk about Elvis and his decline. He asked them if they had ever seen him in concert. Mary begrudgingly said she had seen him about two months ago, in Alabama. Saunders wanted her opinion of the show. Mary said she didn't have anything to compare it too, but she did notice a few fans who were disappointed with the show, and it was evident Elvis had a weight problem. But to her, the show was entertaining and enjoyable even if some fans complained about the brevity and content.

Saunders then said;

"That's just it; the public was unaware of what was going on behind the scene. His negative lifestyle and erratic behavior were taken a toll on him, slowly creeping into his shows making them shorter and less entertaining. His paranoid thoughts were causing him to worry more and more about his popularity. Though he may have been one of the world's greatest entertainers, his insecurity prevented him from believing or accepting it; he seemed to be battling so much personal turmoil he couldn't see the forest for the trees. The sad part of this theory is Elvis thinking the only way to find new life was through death. It may have been the last desperate act of a man on his way out."

Jerry and Lynn were listening intently and were troubled by the notion. Jerry was particularly troubled by it and refused to accept the declining fan base and drug use. He wasn't sure where Saunders was getting his information, but he felt Elvis still had it and his career wasn't in decline. Jerry added; "Maybe Elvis couldn't move like he once did, but hey he was in his 40's, not his 20's."

Saunders agreed;

"Everyone recognized the change in Elvis's stage performance, and it could have been the result of him being in his forties, but Elvis saw himself as a rock n roll star, and that's what he wanted to be. Listen I loved Elvis and sure hope all my suspensions are as crazy as they sound. Hopefully, all this can be put to rest once we view the body."

Though, frustrated Lynn chimed in; "Jerry I hate to say it, but Elvis had not been the same performer for years. You remember that show in Maryland."

Lynn said; "Yeah I remember we thought he was sick he could hardly remember the words to the songs and when he did you could barely understand them."

"He did hold the microphone like a crutch; I don't want to think about that show."

Saunders looked at both asking if they came up with excuses for Elvis's behavior.

"Maybe you blamed it on the flu or possibly just one bad day in the life of a great entertainer. But in truth what you witnessed in Maryland was what thousands of others were seeing. His bizarre behavior the memory losses were evident in several shows. A man can always have a bad show but having an entire tour go to hell. That's time for concern."

Jerry was not pleased with the talk shaking his head and telling Saunders,

"Come on man we are here to celebrate his career and honor his death."

Saunders agreed but then added;

"No one is going to argue that Elvis wasn't a great entertainer, but this led his fans to be more and more demanding. No real fan wants to look at the negative, but in the last couple of years, the negatives have been way too obvious. Fans didn't want to believe it, and neither did Elvis. I feel Elvis had as much trouble handling the criticism as his fans did handling the bad shows. He was facing a true dilemma with his career and life spiraling downhill."

Saunders added fuel to the fire telling them supposedly Elvis had called an old friend last week a Miss Foster who lives in California supposedly one of Elvis's oldest and dearest fans and he tells her he wouldn't be touring. The tour was to begin this week, and he never made any arrangements to cancel or postpone it. Saunders said Elvis told Foster he would not be touring and not to believe anything she hears in the coming weeks he was fine and would just be stepping away from the limelight for a while. Mary did love the creativity of some of these rumors. Roger felt the rumor only added to the speculation.

Roger wanted to know more about Elvis's financial troubles. Saunders said he understood Elvis lost close to ten million dollars on a failed real estate/airplane deal. Mary thought if Elvis were battling depression and anxiety losing 10 million would certainly add to his problems. Saunders excused himself needing to get back to his friends, and Mary asked him to stay in touch and told him how to find her.

After Saunders had left Roger asked Mary her thoughts on all the rumors. Mary didn't see how it could be possible, but Saunders did make a good argument.

"Personally, I feel its pure speculation and some wishful thinking by those not wanting to accept the truth. Even with all the problems I still felt the show I saw was good. Unfortunately, Elvis did look overweight and bloated, but he interacted well with the audience and sounded great."

Roger repeated what she had said; "overweight and bloated was not the review he would have been looking for if he were an entertainer."

Mary then said considering all the negative factors Saunders mentioned Elvis might have been a walking time bomb, and it was just a matter of time before he would fall victim to natural causes no matter how unnatural they were. The time was approaching 4:00 AM and Mary was now feeling the effects of the flight and all the excitement she needed some rest. Soon she would be embarking on a new day of adventure, and she needed to be as fresh as possible.

Mary hoped to catch Lynn and Jerry before they ordered another drink. Both men were struggling with Saunders theories. She caught up with them before they could do any more damage. She told them she needed to get back to the hotel. No one offered resistance. Soon everyone was together driving back to the hotel.

On the way, back, Mary, asked Jerry and Lynn if they had heard anyone else speculating about the death. Jerry said;

"There was a waitress who claimed her cousin saw Elvis downtown about the same time he was pronounced dead, so many rumors who knows what to believe."

At the hotel, most of the action had died down there were a few still hoping to find rooms. Walking through the lobby, Mary heard a lady say she understood Diane Cannon was on her way to Memphis. Mary began to wonder what other celebrities would be coming to Memphis for the funeral. She had heard James Brown was already in town and was making the rounds at some of the clubs. The news reported Ann Margaret who had co-starred with Elvis in a movie would also be attending the funeral. Roger admitted to having a crush on Ann Margret.

Once Mary reached her room though exhausted she knew getting to sleep wouldn't be a certainty. The reporter in her turned on the TV, just in case additional information was available. As she flipped through the channels, she noticed a few stations were showing Elvis movies. One thing she learned while channel surfing was Elvis at one time had been the highest paid actor in Hollywood. His star power reached far beyond the recording industry.

MORE RUMORS

Mary had only gotten a few hours' sleep when she awoke to the sound of the television. She had fallen asleep while watching it earlier. Thet Today Show, Tom Brokaw, and Jane Pauley, reflecting on the career of Elvis and the emotional outcry that had been spawned by his death. Mary again realized how lucky she was to be in Memphis and the middle of the story. She thought just 24 hours earlier she was preparing for a Rotary Club meeting in Dublin Georgia; life can move fast and present some fabulous opportunities.

There was no new information. Considering the pace to get Elvis buried the news regarding the death was painstakingly slow. Maybe it was the circumstances surrounding the death that made the reporting more difficult. Had he died in a plane crash as other rock stars or battled a prolonged illness the news would have been easier to report and accept. But Elvis died unexpectedly and rather unceremoniously. Mary pulled herself away from the coverage knowing she had work to do and took a quick shower.

Once Mary arrived at the grill she spotted Roger enjoying a muffin. Acknowledging her presence by complaining about not being able to get a good cup of tea. Mary smiled and told him when in Rome do as the Romans suggesting he try the coffee. Roger explained he had never quite developed an appreciation for coffee, thus leaving him with a hot cup of water and an unceremonious tea bag. Mary fixed her coffee and told him he didn't know what he was missing.

While waiting for her order, Mary asked Roger if this was his first trip to the states. Roger told her no he had been to the states twice before on business and once for pleasure. Adding; "you would think by now I would've learned to drink coffee." Mary wanted to know about his work assignments in the states. Roger said he'd been very lucky in 64 as a young journalist he was fortunate enough to cover the Beatles first American tour. Telling her; "it was exciting and by all means one of the highlights of my career." Mary was fascinated to learn he had been in the audience when as he put it the boys from Liverpool made quite a statement to the youth of America. Mary was immediately impressed and couldn't hide her excitement; she told him she had watched all three appearances on the Ed Sullivan Show with her parents. Though she was only nine, she still remembers it well. Roger smiled and asked her "Nine huh do you know how old that makes me feel."

Mary said; "that show made quite an impression on me, and to think you covered the Beatles it must have been something."

Roger then added; "Yea I guess you could say I was in the right place at the right time. Sound familiar?"

Mary knew Roger was comparing her circumstances to his earlier assignment. She needed to know, did Roger know any of the Beatles.

"I'm sorry to disappoint you, but no I have been in the same room with them but only for question sessions. I would've loved to have been in their elusive circle of friends, but it just never happened. The limited time I did interact with the group, I found them to be quite friendly and cooperative. But unfortunately, I have no juicy stories to share."

Mary said she was scared to ask about his second assignment? Roger smiled and told her, again the music gods were shining on him when he convinced his editor that he should send him to the states to cover a small music festival in upstate New York called Woodstock. Mary nearly did a spit take she was literally talking to a walking textbook on rock n roll history he covered the Beatles first visit the states, and he covered Woodstock two of the biggest events in her short history with rock n roll. She looked in disbelief saying "Wow Woodstock"? Roger asked; "And how old were you then?" Mary laughed and responded; "fourteen, but who's keeping score." He told her it would be more appropriate to say Woodstock covered him adding that was an assignment he had no interested in ever repeating. Mary said that's a story she would love to hear. Roger indicated press credentials had little value at Woodstock adding it was something and the further removed from it the better his memories get. Roger seemed to be reminiscing when he said;

"It was certainly not your typical assignment, so wild and disorganized, but to the credit of the half million people who made it happen, it was quite a weekend. The music was great the weather awful, and those in attendance made it special. I've considered writing a book about the experience giving an English observers perspective. But I'm afraid I could never truly capture the experience or summarize what took place it was just that bizarre of time. The movie did a decent job covering the feel, but I assure you there are thousands of untold stories."

Roger continued telling her the little reporting he did concern some of the English acts The Who, Joe Cocker, and others. Young musicians who were laying the foundation for what appears to be colorful if not a distinguished career in rock n roll. Roger concluded his Woodstock story by telling her he was young enough to enjoy it and old enough to know better, but it was a highlight. Explaining;

"I feel Woodstock was what many would describe as a perfect storm everything came together to create the ultimate music festival."

Mary told Roger that there had been attempts to duplicate Woodstock, but thus far all had failed to generate the same atmosphere. Roger assured her that was not such a bad thing.

Mary said considering those two assignments she would give him a pass on the coffee. Soon Wayne joined them with camera in hand. Roger greeted Wayne and pointed out the shortcoming of the hotel's tea. Wayne laughed saying he would try the black bottom sorghum or as others call it coffee. Everyone needed a shot of caffeine looking for something to jump start their day.

Shortly Lynn and Jerry joined them they had been down awhile and had already eaten. Both were anxious to get started. Mary asked her rhetorical question "does anyone remember how to get to Graceland?" In unison, everyone replied; "follow the crowds." Jerry said he and Lynn would be waiting in the parking lot. Once again Mary thought the two of them were hard to figure especially Lynn with his jam box offering up his continued musical tribute.

Mary started thinking of Matt Saunders and his theories; he did have some unbelievable ideas and yet made them seemed plausible. She asked Roger if he had given the hoax notion any more thought. Roger said;

"Not really but I do think it makes for a tale suited for the tabloids. These kinds of rumors will sell thousands of papers and possibly books. But I don't put much stock in them."

Both hoped the public viewing would help put the speculation to rest. Both felt time would allow the rumors to melt after all it had only been 24 hours since everyone learned of the death. Mary agreed that the rumors did make for quite a tale but also knew the devil is in the details.

Jerry and Lynn were waiting near the car; both appeared in good spirits as the music sounded from Lynn's jam box. Mary wasn't familiar with the song playing, but Lynn informed her it was a cut from the Love Me Tender album. Wayne placed his camera bag in the truck, and they all piled in and soon were off to Graceland. After a quick stop at Graceland, they hoped to check out Forest Hills Cemetery Elvis's final resting place. The presence of the Shriners was still evident as they passed a group preparing for what appeared to be a parade. Soon they would be driving their funny cars and modified motorcycles all the while wearing their unique headgear and sashes and colorful vest of honor. On any other day, they may have stopped to watch some of the festivities that would surely be entertaining. But today was reserved for Elvis. Mary joked that the Shriners should start offering rides to Graceland in their funny cars, a service many needed. Wayne said now that's a picture he would love to have. Lynn and Jerry remained annoyed by the Shriners; feeling out of respect for Elvis the convention shouldn't continue.

The Shriners weren't the only ones competing for attention in the city; vendors were now present. Vendors of every sort began popping up on street corners, selling T-shirts, posters, photos, records even the Memphis newspaper was selling for five dollars rather than the standard 25 cents. The rule for the day if it had Elvis on it then it was being sold. The activity contributed to the city taking on the appearance of the world's largest outdoor flea market.

A makeshift press conference had begun at Graceland with a family spokesperson addressing the crowds. A tall, slender man, speaking with a southern draw began his remarks by thanking everyone for the wonderful display of love and affection for Elvis. He told the crowd

Elvis would have been impressed and moved by the love shared on this sad occasion. He added that Elvis's family was appreciative for the wonderful flowers and certainly recognized the emotional outcry of the city and the world. Soon he began giving details of the public viewing. Mary sensed a collective sigh of relief when he confirmed there would be a public viewing. He must have sensed the relief of so many when he assured the crowd that the family hoped to accommodate everyone wishing to attend the viewing. An emotional wave engulfed the mourners as he spoke. Soon he began to go over the details once again thanking everyone for their patience's and the tremendous display of love for Elvis and then jokingly apologized for the heat. He told them later in the day Elvis's body would return to Graceland mentioning how much Elvis loved Graceland and his fans. He said the family felt a public viewing at Graceland would be a perfect way to honor both. A section in the mansion was being prepared for the body to lie in state; the mansion doors will open around 3:00 PM for the viewing and the mansion would remain open until 5:00. The limited time didn't set well with the thousands of mourners fearing this would not allow sufficient time for everyone to view the body. Sensing the uneasiness he once again said it was the hope of the family that everyone who wanted to pay their respects would be able to do so.

The viewing would be the first time the mansion had ever been open to the public. It saddened Mary realizing the first public opening of the home would come under such sad circumstances. Before the spokesperson finished with his remarks, fans began to move to the front gate hoping to create a line and wait for the viewing. It would be a long day for sure, and with the high temperature and humidity, it was going to be challenging as well.

Mary was jotting down a few notes when she heard a familiar voice. It was Matt Saunders the investigator saying;

"I see private investigators aren't the only ones who don't sleep."

He was beginning to grow on Mary; he was charming with a winning style. Mary appreciated the ease Saunders interacting with everyone; he didn't take himself or his occupation too seriously. Mary questioned; if he had found any more evidence supporting the hoax theory. He smiled and told her;

"Oh, I keep hearing rumors about rumors who knows what to think. The latest rumors are of who may be responsible for the death that is if he is dead. True or not people are talking and when people talk rumors get spread."

Mary once again wasn't sure Saunders believed the rumors or just enjoyed telling them.

Saunders confirmed the question of the day remained (*How could Elvis be dead*). And he said few wanted to believe the King died on his throne. Saunders apologized for his pun telling Mary it had already been a long day. Mary agreed the rumors weren't helping. Saunders once again reiterated how crazy it sounded but told Mary to remember the line from Mark Twain concerning the exaggeration of his death. Of course, Saunders had no evidence only a gut feeling and an abundance of rumors. Unfortunately, Mary also knew there are no headlines in the gut feeling just a hell of a lot of questions. Saunders said he'd keep an open mind to the possibility and hoped to learn more once he viewed the body. For now, Saunders said he would continue looking into the death that is at least until the next scorned wife called for his services.

He then told Mary of a rumor he was not giving much credence to and that was the body taken to the hospital was a look-alike. Mary was stunned repeating what he had said a look alike. Saunders then said;

"welcomed to the PI world. Believe me; I know this takes the cake for bizarre. But they are saying the man who died was a gentleman who had been working for Presley for the last few months."

Mary shook her head and wondered "are you now talking about murder?"

"No I'm not going that far, but they are saying one of Elvis's stand-ins was terminally ill, and this gave him an opportunity to put the hoax into action. Some are saying with the stand in death; Elvis saw a way to escape his personal prison."

Mary was surprised to learn that Elvis employed some lookalikes. The group of lookalikes were well compensated for their time and were only used to be seen on the grounds of the mansion while Elvis did his thing elsewhere giving him some privacy. The look alike would never have to speak or sing. Saunders felt this theory was the result of some overactive imagination of Elvis's fans.

Mary wondered why Elvis would need a stand-in. Saunders told her to consider stand-ins are used all the time in the movies. With a properly placed stand-in, Elvis would have time to work on his health and his appearance. Something everyone agreed he needed to do. Saunders reminded her it was all speculation and rumors and she could expect them to continue growing. "I'll conduct some interviews and ask a few questions so see what else I can find." Mary laughingly told him he might also want to see if the US landed on the moon as well. Laughing Saunders said she was beginning to think like a private investigator.

Mary was more confused than ever she couldn't tell if Saunders believed in the rumors or was just fanning the flames. She knew the line between reality and fiction was sometimes blurred by details, making her not sure what to think. Saunders told her that you can't always assume red is red or blue is blue it's just the nature of man.

No one knew if the casket would be open or closed at the viewing.

Mary felt certain if it were an open casket then all the speculation could be laid to rest. Her thoughts on the open casket took a hit when Saunders reminded her that a lot depended on how close they allowed the public for the viewing. Nothing was simple with him.

Before leaving Saunders, Mary told him he had given her plenty to think about, and hopefully, she would see him before returning to Georgia. Saunders said; "I've enjoyed sounding these crazy ideas off you, and who knows one day I may need a hotshot journalist to help break the story."

"If any of these rumors do turn out to be true I'm your girl. No matter truth or not they still supply the ingredients to a great tale."

Mary felt a change of venue was in order and decided to do some shopping, and visit some of the vendors across the street from Graceland.

IT'S FOR SALE

A small village of vendors had sprung up across from the mansion. Mary felt business must be good judging, from all the activity. America capitalism was alive and well. Eliminate the flowers, and you would find yourself at one hell of a street festival. Mary was attracted to a purple tent where she decided to make her first stop. The stand offered up a wide variety of T-shirts and considering the ample inventory they were anticipating a big day. The merchant working the stand looked up and asked Mary if she was looking for a T-shirt. Mary told him she did want to get a shirt. But before purchasing one Mary introduced herself as a reporter from Georgia and asked if she could have a few minutes of his time. The vendor told her he could use a break. He introduced himself as Chuck Lawrence and asked what she would like to know? Mary said, "from the look of things you must be expecting a busy day." Chuck looked to be in his early twenties and said; "I certainly hope so." Mary channeling her reporter side asked if he could tell her something about himself. Chuck smiled;

"I'm from Nashville and as you can see in the T-Shirt business. We have a small store front in Nashville, but most of our business comes from selling out of our van at concerts and festivals."

The van parked behind the booth was painted bright yellow and purple with the words (*Say it, Wear it, Share it*) Monkey Breath Tees. Mary asked if he was Mr. Monkey Breath. Chuck laughed and said; "I guess I am. Sounds inviting doesn't it." Though she was interested in the name, she attempted to stay on topic. First, she commented on his inventory of shirts. Chuck acknowledged it was a good thing; demand was high. Chuck said;

"My partner put in some long hours creating these commemorative shirts and others were left over from previous concerts. I was in Atlanta working a Kenny Rogers concert when I learned of the death and drove up after the show. I'm operating on adrenaline and coffee."

Mary wondered if it was the money or Elvis that brought him to Memphis.

"Truthfully it was a little of both noting a man needs to make a living, and I've been following Elvis for nearly three years selling shirts at various shows, and it seemed only right to be here today. I usually put up shop outside the venue and sell shirts and other memorabilia. The last couple of year the sales of Elvis shirts have been slower than usual. But now they were jumping off the shelves."

He excused himself long enough to sell two shirts for twenty dollars. After the sell, Mary asked;

"Do you consider yourself a fan or a businessman."

"I'm a little of both you couldn't do what I do and not have an appreciation for the entertainers, and Elvis was no exception. Sadly, this may be the last opportunity to sell my Elvis products. I guess we could refer to the funeral as his last public appearance. I'll continue to follow other acts selling shirts, but there will never be another Elvis."

Mary said that he sounded like a fan. Lawrence acknowledged

that saying maybe he was after all Elvis had the ability to appeal to everyone especially the common man. They were the fans who shopped his stand looking for the perfect souvenir, and when they bought a T-shirt, they would wear it with pride. Mary then said she hated being such a reporter but had to ask if he were going to miss the entertainer or the business. Lawrence then said he would miss the man more than the dollar but don't get him wrong he would also miss the money. Mary thanked him for his honesty and then asked him about Elvis's career, she told him she had heard people say Elvis was losing his appeal; everything she had seen or read lately would indicate his career was on a downhill slide. She asked if he saw it that way. Lawrence said,

"Unfortunately, that's probably a fair assessment he was not the entertainer he used to be, but he still gave a hell of a show. Like I said sales had dropped off. Not sure why it could have been the result of declining popularity due to shorter shows or the health problems. "I've spoken to a few of his older fans some this morning, and all seemed to be reminiscing about the early years when Elvis could make a room come to life. One man had told me Elvis had the ability to energize everyone who came to see him perform. There had to have been a lot of pressure. His fans all wanted him to be more like his younger self; it had to have been draining. The man was loved, and that love produced a lot of pressure and responsibility."

Lawrence seemed to be contemplating his thoughts when he said;

"I guess no one shouldn't have been surprised by the death. Hine site would suggest it was just a matter of time. That's what makes it so sad. It didn't take a rocket scientist to see the man was struggling and he was being taken down by a negative lifestyle, and yet no one did anything about it. In life things, can happen that we don't think are possible and the death of Elvis is one of those moments. Even with his problematic behavior and reported drug use, it's still hard to accept, sometimes facing the truth can be a challenge. I guess that sounds a bit odd coming from a someone making money on the tragedy. But business aside I didn't want to believe the reports, and I'd give all the money back if the reports were just a bad dream."

Mary asked if he had heard any rumors about the death not being true but a hoax designed to give Elvis some time off. Lawrence replied;

"Oh, I've heard them alright there are plenty going around. I had one customer report Elvis was spotted coming out the back side of the hospital under tight security; another claimed to have seen him at Graceland hours after learning of the death. But I'm sure they are just rumors some that just happen to be insane. I don't put any credit to them Elvis is gone, and it's a shame, but he's dead. Just look at everything you see is a tribute to a falling star most of those here today are fans, and that should tell you something about Elvis and his popularity."

Mary said she just didn't understand why there were so many rumors. Lawrence said that's human nature consider it this way if Elvis could die, then anyone could die. Lawrence reminded her that many viewed Elvis as being larger than life, and such thought will create a need for an alternative reality. Both agreed that those who refuse to believe he's dead might not be in touch with reality.

Lawrence finally said;

"I like a good conspiracy theory as much as the next guy, but the notion that he faked his death was just too stupid and way too farfetched. But I'm a businessman, I've thought about a new T-Shirt design something like Elvis surrounded by clouds gripping a microphone."

Mary laughed and said she felt it would be a hit. She then thanked him for his time and said she should get a souvenir shirt while she was there. Lawrence told her to pick one out free of charge. Mary thanked him again and asked what he had in a medium. Lawrence then pulled out a white shirt with a young Elvis awarding a scarf to an adoring fan. Mary offered to pay him, but he told her to consider it a gift to the press. To which Mary told him the press thanks you.

Leaving Monkey Breath T's Mary couldn't help but be impressed with the ever-growing number of mourners now surrounding the grounds and mansion. The only thing rivaling the number of mourners were the mountains of flowers lining the streets and gates. There were small teddy-bears with cards and signs wishing Elvis peace. Almost every arrangement imaginable was on display. As you would expect there were floral arrangements made to resemble guitars and treble cliffs symbolizing his music. From single red roses to full bouquets, various colors and varieties of flowers paved the streets. The floral business was booming. You could find hound dogs and blue suede shoes, even a hound dog wearing blue suede shoes. It was something to see. Anything to honor Elvis and his legacy some quite beautiful and others just plain tacky no matter your taste you could find it on display in the thousands of flowers laid at the gates of Graceland.

After Mary had caught back up with Roger and Wayne, they decided to visit the press section and speak with some other reporters. Roger noticed her T-shirt and commented on it. Mary showed him the shirt and said it was a gift for good journalism. Roger just laughed. Mary slapped him on the arm and told him to be nice, and suggested he get one noting every good trip should include a souvenir.

Shortly after noon, the Hearst arrived at Graceland. Turning into one of the side entrances of the mansion to avoid most of the mourners, gathered at the front gate. Few could get a glimpse of the

Hearst as it prepared to unload the casket. Some of the fans began to run toward the gate, and others attempted to jump the barrier fence that surrounded the property. Security had little trouble preventing anyone from getting onto the grounds. The sight of the casket caused some to start crying once again with a few sobbing uncontrollably. The reality of Elvis's death was once again striking home.

Roger learned that plans were still in place to open the mansion around 3:00 PM for the public viewing and unfortunately it didn't look as if the press would get any special treatment. The officer told Roger the viewing would take place in the foyer of the mansion; where Elvis would lie in state underneath a crystal chandelier. Wayne said he heard the chandelier had some significance to Elvis supposedly one of his favorite possession. The public would enter through the front were two large stone lions guarded the entrance. Once in the mansion, it was their understanding that the mourners would follow a small hallway into the foyer and exit out a side entrance, allowing for quick and orderly movement. White linens would accent the pathway.

With the casket now in the mansion another strange phenomenon began to take place, every so often a limousine would pull up only to be turned away by security. Mary learned people were renting limousines hoping to get through the gates so they could get into the mansion possibly passing off as an invited guest. It was a nice try but not a successful one. Mary felt it was just another example, of people making money off the funeral.

Before the viewing, Roger and Mary decided to get something to eat; they found a small diner located in the strip mall across from Graceland. On the way to the diner, the solitude of the occasion was interrupted by a lady looking to be in her mid-40's running down the street hysterically screaming that she was Elvis's wife and she needed to see him. She was of course dressed in black and causing quite a scene when a uniform police officer grabbed her and quickly escorted her off. Mary said; "a hidden wife who knew the way things were going we are liable to see Elvis's dead twin brother."

Roger was surprised to learn of the twin who died at birth. Mary told him that some speculated the loss of the twin brother was the reason Elvis was so close to his mother. Roger said; "For someone who says she's not a fan she seemed to know a lot about Elvis and his life." Mary got a dig in telling him it was not a fan but just good journalism. Roger smiled.

As they waited to enter the Tavern a small Mom and Pop operation that was doing a rousing business, Mary was forced to fess up. Unfortunately, she couldn't take much credit for knowing about the brother she just learned about him herself. Roger wondered if there were any other siblings. Mary explained to him the brother who died at birth was the only one, but it is probably a safe bet the lady proclaiming to be his secret wife would not be the only one making an appearance.

Once seated Roger asked if there was an American delicacy Mary could recommend. Mary told him to stick with the special, or they may be there all day, and they didn't want to miss any of the excitement. Both ordered the day's special meatloaf potatoes and green beans a true southern meal. While waiting for the meal they began discussing the funerals schedule taking place the next day at 2:00 PM.

At lunch, Mary asked Roger his thoughts on Elvis. Thinking the English perspective would be a little different from that of the American fan. She told Roger some of Elvis's fans blamed the English music invasion on Elvis's declining popularity. Roger agreed that there might be some truth in that but also said Elvis was not the only act affected by the invasion. The music industry is a tough business, and it's not easy staying on top no matter who you are. Blaming the British invasion on Elvis's decline may be a convenient excuse for a down period in American music. Roger told her when he traveled with the Beatles in the early sixties; Elvis was quite popular, and the Beatles admired him.

Mary told Roger of a radio station in her hometown taking calls on who was better Elvis or the Beatles and one of her friends though only nine at the time called the station and told them there were four Beatles and only one Elvis, so the Beatles were four times better.

Roger then added;

"Don't get me wrong I certainly did have an appreciation for Elvis and his music. No one could deny Elvis impact on the entertainment industry. The man was a cornerstone of Rock N Roll history. It's going to take awhile for everyone to understand the true impact of Elvis's career. Elvis's legacy will live it in the music he left behind."

Mary wondered how Roger would describe Elvis showmanship. Roger told her;

"Elvis had the quality to take ownership of a song. When he sang, you knew it was him, and his interpretation left little for the imagination, and people loved that. He had a soulful connection to the lyrics making the listener feel that he was the only one capable of singing the song. His stage presence was just a bonus. I remembered reading from a show Elvis did in New York attended by Lennon and McCartney and several other artists. The reviewer wrote even though the crowd included several of rock's nobility, it was Elvis who was king. To me what made Elvis the King was his ability to make the casual listener feel special as if they were being singled out leaving the audience wanting more."

Mary considered what Roger said, and she knew he was right Elvis could transform his music into entertainment, from the silly to the sublime. She asked Roger if he had a favorite song, a song that would make you stop and listen if only for a moment. Roger said he was a sucker for (Can't Help Falling in Love). Mary smiled and told Roger to be careful he was beginning to show a tender side.

Soon they were on their way back to the mansion before crossing Elvis Presley Boulevard; they stopped at one of the vendors, where Roger purchased a hand-held fan with a black and white photo of Elvis singing and the words "The King is Dead" and "Long Live the King" surrounding the picture. The fan was a needed commodity with the sweltering heat serving two purposes one honoring Elvis and the other a way to fight the heat. It would be two hours before the viewing would begin.

The mountain of flowers and the thousands of fans now occupied most of the space around the mansion. A van with the lettering Lila's Flowers, Collierville TN pulled up making another flower drop. The family was not accepting any more flowers in the home and were asking for deliveries placed outside the gate. Mary tried to catch up with the driver before he could leave, hoping to ask him a few questions. The driver looked to be a high school student possibly working a summer job. Mary felt he may have been a little overwhelmed by everything, but he was willing to talk. Mary stating the obvious said he looked as if he had been very busy. The young man told her it was the busiest day he'd had ever seen. Adding it was crazy around their shop and yet the orders keep coming. His boss was certainly enjoying the boom in business. He told Mary that most of the shops around town were having difficulty keeping up with the demand and his shop was officially out of flowers and wasn't sure when another order would arrive. Mary asked who was making the orders. "We're getting orders from all over. A friend of mine at another larger shop in Memphis told me they had received an order from Russia. But he was more impressed with the fact that an order from Elton John had come in."

Once Mary finished talking with the flower delivery boy, she began looking for Jerry and Lynn. She found them camped out close to the front gate. Both anxious for the viewing. Putting her reporter hat on she went up to them. She just wanted to talk to them but didn't want anyone to think she was breaking in line. Lynn laughing told her the limousine parade had continued and most turned away. Jerry told Mary the spokesperson returned to reassure everyone that the doors would be opening soon and the viewing would begin shortly.

Mary felt the crowd was struggling with their emotions, not knowing what to think or how to act. More than a few gave the appearance they were walking on egg shells not sure what to do. A few mourners had become overcome by a combination of emotions and the temperature, some requiring assistance. The police had been kept busy handing out water to combat the heat but could offer little help when it came to the emotions. Those who needed medical attention were for the most part suffering from dehydration.

Shortly after 3:00 PM the front doors of the mansion swung opened and uniformed security guards moved to the front gate. One of the guards carried with him a bullhorn to address the crowd. Before giving any instructions, he once again told everyone how much the family appreciated the outpouring of love for Elvis. Soon he began to tell everyone to line up asking for the line to be two across falling in behind the front gate. He assured everyone that they would be able to enter the mansion. He then gave directions they would enter through the front doors and once inside please be respectful and move quickly to allow everyone the opportunity to say good-bye. Once the line began to form the guards opened the gate, and the procession began. The mourners passed by the large lions; as they made their way into the mansion. It was a slow but steady process. From Mary's vantage point she could tell the crowd was well behaved and it looked like the security staff would have few problems.

Mary and Roger decided to wait to get into line hoping to see Lynn and Jerry once they went through the procession. Lynn's appearance was a bit different he had been instructed to leave his jam box behind. One of the police officers at the front allowed Lynn to leave it with him until he passed through the mansion. Lynn and Jerry would be among the first ones in and Mary looked forward to getting their reaction. As Lynn and Jerry made their way into the mansion, Mary and Roger went to the far side to wait for them to emerge from the viewing. The viewing was well on its way and appeared to be orderly.

When Lynn and Jerry exited the mansion, both seemed shaken; Lynn spoke first saying he didn't believe that was Elvis adding that he wasn't even sure it was a body. Jerry said he didn't know who it was but he was sure it wasn't Elvis. Mary tried to understand what they were saying. They told Mary the body favored Elvis, but neither felt confident it was him. They told her the body wore one of the famed jumpsuits, but that was the only certainty they had. Mary tried to explain this by telling them that it could be the result of the makeup used in preparing the body. Jerry seemed to like this explanation and told her she might be right.

As Mary spoke with the pair, she saw medical personnel entering the side entrance and later learned that it was to assist a few mourners who had fainted on the inside when they passed the coffin. Again, the emotion and the heat were the culprits. The crowds were moving quickly, and she felt she and Roger would have no trouble getting in. Those walking out of the mansion appeared rather stoic and reserved. She did hear several say that it didn't look like Elvis some even saying the body was a fake and they knew it. It was time for Roger and

Mary to get in line. Wayne knew he would not be allowed in with his camera, so he remained outside taking a photo of the procession.

Soon it was 5:00 PM but the doors remained open. Vernon Presley, Elvis's father, was persuaded to leave the doors open for an additional thirty minutes so hopefully, everyone would be able to get through the line. Roger and Mary needed the extra time, and fortunately, they would be able to get into the mansion after 5:00.

Once through the doorway, you were greeted by a scarlet carpeted hall that led to a large foyer in the mansion where the coffin sat. In an area near the coffin, you could see white and gold folding chairs placed where the actual funeral would take place. A brightly gleaming copper coffin was open showing the mourners the body of Elvis. As Mary gazed at his swollen face with sideburns nearly reaching his chin, she understood how Lynn and Jerry could feel the corpse was not that of Elvis. The body gave the impression that he was at rest and composed not the high-energy entertainer everyone remembered. It looked more like a painted manikin of Elvis. Of course, very few had seen Elvis at rest, and this may have been the reason some refused to believe it was him. His face looked molded from wax and with the heat, it seemed to glisten. As Mary made her way past the casket, she heard a lady say it didn't look like Elvis repeating this to one of her companions that he just didn't look like himself. Some of the mourners just stood by the coffin and sobbed needing to be moved along by security.

Before leaving the foyer, Mary surveyed as much of the mansion she could hoping to gain an understanding of how Elvis lived. The plantation-style mansion was very ornate and decorative showing an opulence that surprised Mary. The visible furniture appeared to be oversized, from the mahogany dining table to the satin covered chairs everything seems to scream a statement of grandeur. The entrance to the dining room from the foyer marked with floor to ceiling scarlet drapes tied with gold tassels. Looking beyond the casket, she could see a clear glass nude statue; that gave her the impression Elvis had had some unusual taste. Though they were only in the mansion for a moment, it made a lasting impression on both. Roger withheld any comments while in the mansion, but once they were out, he leaned over whispering that was some show. Mary told him to hush and reminded him to be careful; if he offended some of these fans, she was quite certain even his charming accent would not be much of defense for the wrath of an angry Elvis fan. Now was not the time to be making jokes about the king or his home.

Once back outside Mary took the opportunity to speak to a group of fans she learned were from Birmingham AL. They were all pleased that they could pay their respects. One said it was just so hard to believe Elvis was gone. Mary asked what they would remember about the day. An older lady said she would remember being in Graceland with Elvis, not the way she had hoped, but that's what she would remember. One fan told Mary she was impressed with the flowers having never seen so many; saying she hoped to pick a few up to add to her collection of Elvis memorabilia. The ladies appeared to be enjoying themselves even during the sad time. Everyone was celebrating and mourning in their way. While Mary was talking to the fans when Wayne came over to tell her, he had seen Matt Saunders, and she may want to talk with him again. Wayne said it appears Saunders has, even more, questions than answers after viewing the body.

Mary found Saunders speaking to a security guard by one of the side gates. They didn't appear to be talking about Elvis just friendly conversation. Once Saunders noticed Mary, he turned his attention to her. Mary asked his thoughts on the viewing. Saunders shook his head and told Mary;

"I hate to say it, but the viewing only adds to my suspicions. I especially didn't like how they herded everyone like cattle giving no one any real time to study the body."

Mary reminded him that there was a need to accommodate thousands of fans in a short period. He acknowledged this;

"I know, but it just felt they were trying to hide something. Maybe I'm reading too much into it but it's almost like they hoped to prevent anyone from getting a good look at the body. The distance and the quickness of the line left me with more questions. I'm afraid my cynical side has emerged. The little time they gave us only adds to my speculations making me more skeptical of the whole thing."

He then asked Mary if she was able to walk through the procession. Mary told him she had, but she still hadn't processed it yet. Smiling Saunders said;

"You must think I'm crazy. If so you wouldn't be the first nor the last; it comes with the job. But I just feel the body didn't appear to be Elvis and to top it off the body looked to be sweating, and dead people don't sweat."

Mary agreed the body did seem to have a gleam to it but felt that may have been the results of the lighting.

One thing Mary was certain of was the surreal feeling created by the viewing. If they had put a wax replica in the casket, it was a good one. But Mary was holding on to the belief that the body was indeed Elvis. Before she left Saunders, she told him once again if he should find out anything newsworthy to please give her a call. They both laughed, and Saunders agreed to keep her informed.

Mary caught up with the others, she Roger and Wayne was ready for something different. As they prepared to leave, a light shower began to fall only adding to the muggy feeling. Mary again wondered what Elvis would have thought about the circus atmosphere surrounding his funeral. From the vendors to the flowers and the incredible lines it was something to behold. Few had left Graceland most of the crowd would be staying for the night holding their personal vigil. Those that did leave would surely be back in the morning to watch the funeral procession.

Roger had a chance to talk with the family spokesman and had gotten additional information about the funeral. Following the viewing, they would move the coffin back into the main living room where the funeral would take place at 2 pm the next day. Per his source, nearly 200 people had been invited to the ceremony. The limited space obviously limited the number of invites. An interesting fact Roger learned was Elvis's casket was a replica of the one used for his mother's funeral. The casket was lined with copper and contained a four-inch stainless steel cylinder for identification purposes if the remains were exhumed and identified. This little bit of trivia intrigued Roger not knowing if this was routine. Once the funeral service was complete, the body would then be placed in a Mausoleum at Forest Hills Cemetery were intermit would take place. They also planned to move thousands of flowers from the street to the grounds of the cemetery.

Soon the funeral would be over, and everyone would be returning to their homes. Wayne said he needed to fly out that night he had responsibilities in London that needed his attention. Roger would be staying through the service and then heading back to Nashville. In Nashville, he hoped to attend the Saturday night show at the Grand Ole Opry and fly home Sunday morning. Roger felt the show would include a tribute to Elvis. He was curious to how the Opry would choose to honor Elvis.

When Roger spoke of the Grand Ole Opry, it made Mary wonder if Elvis every played the Opry. Roger was pleased that he did know something about Elvis and the Opry. He told her Elvis did play the Opry early in his career possibly in 54. And it was his understanding it was the only time Elvis played the Opry. Supposedly Elvis's style didn't set well with the Opry regulars or management, and his performance was not well received even to the point that someone with the Opry suggested Elvis not give up his day job. Mary wondered if someone did say that or was it an urban legion. Roger said no matter Elvis never, returned to the Opry.

The information Roger had on the Opry and Elvis impressed Mary another reason to respect his work and his research. She could see why he wrote for a major paper. She was fortunate to have met both Roger and Wayne.

Wayne had arranged a flight to New York where he would catch a flight to London. Lynn and Jerry were not interested in going to the airport and said they would catch up with them later.

Before Mary had a chance to leave Jerry asked about her thoughts of the viewing. Mary said she wasn't sure what to think, but it seemed a fair number of people were still questioning the whole thing. Lynn then added he was one of them saying as a follower of Elvis's career he was having trouble believing that was him in the casket. But he still couldn't comprehend how anyone could or would fake their death. No one knew the answer. Jerry felt if the viewing was a fake then they certainly could have done a better job. He felt Elvis would not have been pleased with the way he looked. Jerry added that on stage Elvis was so alive, it's hard to imagine him lying in a casket.

Mary suggested;

"those feelings may simply be a result of the fan in everyone. I've been racking my brain over it all day. Here's a crazy scenario; if Elvis was dead and they used a wax figure, it would only add to the speculation and talk. And in the entertainment business, talk means sales and sales mean money. It would also give the fans who refuse to believe he's dead something to hold on to thinking one day he would return to the stage, and this nightmare would be over."

Lynn shook his head and said:

"Gee's next thing you're going to say is Elvis is vacationing with Jimmy Hoffa or Marylyn Monroe."

Mary told him that was the beauty of rumors you can put anything out there, and it's up to the audience to accept it or reject it. With such a large fan base for Elvis, almost any rumor would find an audience and continue to grow. And when the legend of Elvis grows record sells will follow, Mary felt it was quite ingenious.

Lynn didn't like the talk about Elvis faking his death and told Mary that was not the way Elvis operated, adding Elvis was an honest and decent man. Mary acknowledged she might be getting caught up in the conspiracy theories, but it was still food for thought. She added. Hopefully, rational thinking will win out, and the family could peaceably lay Elvis to rest, doing so on their terms without the public screaming for more proof.

On the way to the airport, Mary wondered if Wayne had gotten enough photos. Wayne shook his head and told her he had photos of photos. He acknowledged he felt he had some great shots, telling her he even had photos of the Shriners and their funny miniature cars, these photos were for his personal collection. Wayne said he had enjoyed Memphis more than he expected noting the Shriners had supplied a little aversion from the funeral with their partying attitude. Mary agreed and told him this is a reflection of the south, southerners mourn, and southerner's party sometimes at the same time and sometimes because of the other.

Once they reached the airport, Mary decided to check on a flight home. Her adventure was coming to an end soon she would return to her old duties of handling the obits in Dublin and reporting on the Ramblings on Main Street.

Wayne had a flight on Eastern back to New York soon the group would be down to four, though Wayne was the toughest to figure Mary knew she would still miss him. Before he boarded, Mary gave him her address and asked if he would send her some of his photos. Wayne said it would be an honor and thanked her for her hospitality and for helping make the experience enjoyable.

Once they saw Wayne off, Mary checked on flights back to Georgia. Piedmont Airlines appeared to be her best bet with a flight leaving around 8:30 PM the next day for Macon. Macon was about 70 miles from Dublin she felt her roommate Sherrie would be willing to make the drive. If everything went as scheduled, she would arrive in Macon around 11:00. If all went well on traveling home, she would have time to construct and file her story for Friday's edition. Before booking the flight, she called Sherrie. Luckily, she agreed to meet Mary at the airport excited to hear about the adventure.

After booking the flight Mary and Roger were both ready for something different. Roger suggested finding a restaurant featuring some of Memphis's famed Bar B Q his treat. Mary told him he had a lot of southern charm for an Englishman. Roger took it as a compliment but confessed his desire for Bar B Q was a result of all the advertising proclaiming Memphis the Bar BQ capital of the world. Mary told him she couldn't speak for the Memphis style Bar B Q, but both Georgia, and South Carolina had their share of famed Bar B Q joints. They agreed a taste of Memphis was in order.

THE BRIGHTWOOD

A LARGE BILLBOARD OUTSIDE THE AIRPORT suggested the Brightwood for famed Memphis Bar B Que, and luckily it was on the road back to Graceland. (*The Brightwood Rib Joint*) *Where fine dining and country, eating meet.* The Brightwood was a large wooden structure resembling an old farm house. Outside was a short line waiting to enter. Obviously, they were not alone in the desire for some of Memphis's finest Bar B Que.

Once they joined the quickly moving line, Mary noticed a gentleman waiting who must have been a local celebrity of some kind the way others kept speaking to him. His shirt gave the call letters WMTE with the slogan "*is on your side!*" He overheard Mary and Roger discussing the Bar B Que when he began telling them they had made a great decision and it would be well worth the short wait. Mary wanted to know more about the man and began a conversation with him first asking if he had any recommendations. He told her she couldn't beat the combo platter, featuring pulled pork and ribs; comes with coleslaw and your choice of potato he gave it his full endorsement. He also suggested they order the sweet tea saying it was worth its weight in gold. Roger told him he wasn't sure about sweet tea. The man not to be deterred simply said; "well partner if you don't like the Brightwood's sweet tea you'll never learn to like sweet tea." Mary laughing tells Roger he should try it. Roger stated with such a ringing endorsement how could he say no.

The man was so outgoing and pleasant that Roger and Mary asked if he would like to join them for dinner. Mary felt if he did work for a local TV station it would give her a chance to pick his brain about the funeral and possibly some of the rumors.

Dan Hoops of WMTE introduced himself and said he would love to join them. Mary asked if he was a reporter. Hoops replied he was and that it had been a zoo with the death of Elvis and the Shriners in town. Hoops asked if they were in Memphis for work or pleasure. Mary extended her hand and gave her name and said she was a reporter for a small paper in Georgia. Roger then shook Hoops' hand telling him his name and that he worked for the London Mirror. Hoops was, impressed with Rogers place of employment, repeating the name of the paper. In somewhat of a turnaround, Hoops asked Roger if he could get a short interview with him for the station. He felt Roger could help demonstrate the global appeal of Elvis? Mary smiling interjected she was disappointed that Dublin wasn't global enough. He knew she was joking and just smiled and said; "you did say Georgia, not Ireland right."

Hoops asked when they arrived and how were they finding Memphis. Both responded "busy." Mary told him they arrived the day before adding that she was in Georgia working the obituary desk and Roger was in Nashville when they learned the news. Hoops said things could change rapidly. He then shifted his attention to Roger, wondering why he was in Nashville. Roger gave him his reason and added that country music was quite popular in England, so it seemed a good time to do a feature on the home of Country music. Hoops jokingly said; so, the U.S. gives England country music and England, in turn, gives the U. S. the Beatles and the Stones. Roger smiled telling Hoops it may not have been exactly a fair trade but surprisingly country music was very popular in England especially some of the older traditional acts. He began to name some of the acts including Bill Anderson, Slim Whitman, George Jones and Johnnie Cash. All considered superstars in England. Learning this Hoops tells him his timing was perfect getting two stories for the price of one. Roger acknowledged that there was something to being in the right place at the right time.

Soon they were seated as Mary glanced around she thought the crowd looked to be a mix of locals and tourist. It was easy to identify the locals most of them recognized Hoops and were saying hello, a few asking questions about the station's coverage of the funeral. As a rule, they were polite, but Mary sensed they wanted to ask him more questions about the death. The death and funeral were dominating most of the conversations. With the number of mourners and press in town, Memphis was the epicenter for the death.

Their waitress a somewhat overweight girl whose name tag read Tammy welcomed them to the Brightwood. Tammy knew Hoops speaking to him as if he were an old friend it seemed the Brightwood was one of his favorite spots. And it didn't hurt that Hoops was a local TV personality adding to his recognition. Tammy looked over at Mary and Roger and asked if they were with the station as well. Before anyone could answer, Hoops told her that today The Brightwood was hosting the national press. Mary here is from the Georgia Press, and Roger is with the London press core. Mary told the waitress they were in town for the funeral. Roger smiled, and once he spoke, it was easy to see Tammy was fascinated with the accent immediately saying, so you are from London. Roger grinning told her London was home. Tammy quickly told Roger, "Sugar I just love your accent." Roger was flattered. She then said; "I feel an English accent just oozed reassurance." It was clear Tammy would have stayed and talked to Roger for a while if he hadn't said;

"Dan tells us the Brightwood is one of the best places in town do you have any recommendations."

Tammy echoed Hoops suggestion;

"You can't go wrong with the ribs. That's all Dan orders the combo plate with extra ribs. Dan interrupted by saying; "why stop a good thing." Tammy smiled and said; "it's all good at the Brightwood."

"Well if that's the case bring me the combo and a glass of that famed sweet tea," Tammy assured him he wouldn't be disappointed the southern charm was dripping from her lips Mary ordered the same. Hoops ordered his usual. Once Tammy left the table, Mary suggested Roger may have a new fan. Roger was a little embarrassed with the comments but took it in stride saying sometimes the accent served him well.

While waiting for their food, Hoops asked them if they had any time to enjoy Memphis. Mary said; "unfortunately, we have only seen little of Memphis, but they did get down to Beal St. earlier. I'm just happy to be here."

Roger said he loved the diversity the city offered. Dan said that's Memphis and he was glad they were finding it inviting.

Mary inquired about Dan's thoughts of the death. Hoops said;

"I feel the best way to sum it up is Elvis was a local boy who happened to be a national icon. National icons don't die every day. But I don't think it should have been considered unexpected even at 42 considering Elvis's lifestyle. But still, it's difficult to accept. Elvis had been part of our community and culture for nearly twenty-five years, and in a blink of an eye, he's gone. His influence far outstretched the boundaries of Memphis, yet he was still considered a hometown boy. The magnitude of his popularity and the love his fans shared is now on display throughout the city. Roger, I bet your paper didn't have a representative for the funeral of Otis Redding or Janis Joplin. No, the death of Elvis is a story that affects the world and demands worldwide coverage."

Mary began telling Hoops about Saunders the private investigator and his speculation that the death may be a ruse and the whole thing could have been orchestrated to give Elvis a way out from a demanding public. As a local newsman, Mary felt Hoops would have a better perspective on the rumors than she or Roger. Hoops admitted it was a crazy idea, but he had certainly heard it. Hoops wondered if the PI had given any reasons for the scam. Before she could answer, he told them the story line of Elvis wanting to get away from a demanding public, but personally, he believed fans in denial were fueling this rumor. Hoops didn't feel there was much substance to the rumors and figured most were the result of an over imaginative public blindsided by the news no one wanted to accept. Hoops felt there are times people don't want to accept the truth, and then they look for alternatives that may be more acceptable.

Hoops continue telling Mary and Roger that he felt there was no denying that Elvis's celebrity status had taken its toll. Elvis was showing signs of wilting under pressure. Mary said that's just it the investigator said the same thing, and because of this pressure, he felt the rumors may have some merit. Hoops chuckled, telling Mary that her investigator friend certainly had an active imagination, but he felt the rumors were just that, rumors. Hoops just couldn't believe a man even of Elvis wealth could pull off such a hoax. Hoops added he had followed Elvis's career for several years and personally felt Elvis was as dependent on his celebrity status as he was painkillers. Elvis needed his fans, and from the look of things, his fans needed him.

Mary questioned what would be the benefit of such rumors. Hoops said simply

"it keeps the legend alive. Records will continue to sell, and movies will continue to play. And if we are talking about Elvis, he will continue to live. You may be too young to remember, but after President Kennedy assassination there were plenty of rumors. There were some who believed the President didn't die, but his wounds put him into a vegetative state. So, to protect the government from a major disruption and save the citizens the pain of such an event death was the easiest thing to sell. And the rumors only got worse; after Jackie, remarried supposedly, allowing for Kennedy to be moved to a small Greek island to live out the remainder of his life."

Mary not wanting to change the subject from Elvis wondered if Hoops knew of any money problems Elvis may have had. Hoops told her he understood Elvis had some bad real-estate investments losing possibly millions of dollars. But that doesn't go away with death. Mary confirmed Hoops didn't put any stock in the rumors. Hoops told her;

"I feel Elvis is dead, and unfortunately for his adoring public, he died in a very bizarre fashion. The weight issues, the drug use all tend to support the fact that the death is real. And if you were going to fake your death wouldn't you come up with a better story. I did cover a story a few years ago, where a man faked his death in a boating accident. Most people felt he was dead that was until he was seen at Disneyworld a couple of years later. Those who refused to believe Elvis is dead will cling to these theories and rumors but not me. For some, the truth hurts, and in this case, the truth is Elvis is dead."

"It was the PI's notion that in death Elvis's popularity would enjoy a revival and from what you're saying you may agree with that."

"I do believe in death Elvis will enjoy a resurgence of popularity, dead or alive this funeral will do more for his career than anyone could imagine. There are plenty of examples where careers live on long after the death. It's only natural it's what fans do. Death gives the fans of Elvis the power to remember him the way they want to. Fans can create their memories not having reality spoil it."

Roger wondered if Hoops felt Elvis would be as big a star in death as he was alive. "He may not be as big, but he certainly going to remain a star, it would be hard to be any bigger than he was in his early years. But I'm confident that Elvis's career will enjoy a resurgence bringing wealth to his estate for years to come. Even though his fame was beginning to erode society is a forgiven bunch, and that forgiveness will come with a reenergized memory of Elvis and his star power. Elvis may not have faked his death, but he did pick a pretty good time to die considering how his career was going."

Mary shook her head sarcastically and thanked Hoops for that upbeat report. Hoops just smiled and told her he was preparing her for the next twenty to thirty years in the saga of Elvis Aaron Presley.

Tammy soon brought the food and with its arrival Hoops proclaimed now here is a story with truly a happy ending. Tammy wondered if Dan had been behaving. Mary explained that Hoops had been sharing his thoughts on Elvis and his legacy. Mary asked if Tammy had any thoughts on the death.

Tammy said;

"Everyone is going to miss him that's for sure. But fortunately, he left us with his music and movies. I want to remember him in his early years when he ruled the music scene not just in Memphis but throughout the world. Those were some great years for Memphis and Elvis."

Roger asked if she was a big fan. Tammy smiled and told him she was one of the biggest and she would always love his music. She felt there would never be another Elvis.

Once Tammy left the table, Dan said Tammy's a sweet girl a hard worker who enjoys people, she's a typical fan. She knew what she liked about the man, and she didn't allow negative factors to change her opinion. Soon everyone was busy eating no time for talk.

The Bar B Que was different from what Mary had known in SC or Georgia, but it was good, and it did carry a punch. She thanked Dan for his suggestion and said he was right about the tea. Roger seemed to be enjoying the food and even learning to drink the ice tea.

Though Dan didn't find any reason to believe the rumors Mary felt he did offer up a good argument to consider why someone would entertain faking his death. The most compelling, being how in death many careers are resurrected. It was true others had found fame in death. James Dean was considered a legendary actor following his death. Buddy Holly became Rock n Roll royalty. Who became immortalized in song and film? Elvis would be no different his career would be remembered for good and the bad would be forgotten or at least forgiven.

Finishing up their meal, Tammy made one more round asking if they had saved room for some of their famous banana pudding. Roger told Dan he failed to mention the pudding. Hoops said it good but he seldom had room for it after feasting on the ribs and Bar BQ. Everyone kindly rejected the pudding though it did sound inviting.

Mary asked Dan to recommend a place they could go that night, somewhere that wouldn't all be tourist or Shriners. Dan told her she might be asking the impossible. He did, however, suggest they check out a place called Mama's Money. It's a club that features a wide range of music and some dancing and from what he understood it was a favorite of the University crowd.

Roger and Mary were pleasantly surprised when Dan asked if they had any interest in seeing the Mausoleum where Elvis would be entombed. He told them he would be doing a feed for the morning show and would love for them to come out for it. Even though it meant arriving early in the morning, the idea appealed to both. Neither hesitated to say yes. Hoops told them where to meet the next morning, and ask they arrive around 7:00 AM. Mary thought it sounded great adding to her lucky streak. Hoops confessed his invitation might be a little self-serving thinking it would be nice to have some others in the shot while doing the feed. He also hoped to get an interview with them if possible. They both said no problem and Mary added that they might even have more rumors to discuss. Hoops smiled telling her he was certain they had just scraped the surface on the rumor mill.

Once back at Graceland Mary and Roger observed a sincere effort was underway to organize a candlelight vigil for the night. The scene at Graceland would remain with Mary for some time. The worship some of the fans were displaying bothered her. Elvis, after all, was just a man and a man with his share of faults. Maybe her age was showing, but she was having a tough time relating, to the shedding of all the tears. The whole scene made her question society. Why do people become so wrapped up in celebrities and their lives? Is it a desire to have the lifestyle of a celebrity or maybe it's an outgrowth of something deeper and more disturbing? Mary felt the type of worship she was witnessing was in direct conflict with what is taught in the bible especially the commandment Thou Shall Have no Other Gods before Me.

Maybe she was a little too judgmental, but that didn't keep her from questioning society and the way it treats celebrities. She questioned whether she was not being fair to the thousands of mourners where did she come off judging others. She told Roger her concerns; Roger said he felt she was too analytical feeling what they were witnessing was little more than people getting caught up in the drama allowing their emotions to play off each other. He assured her all in all what they were seeing was common when someone of great popularity dies. Mary welcomed Rogers view.

When they got back to Graceland, they located Lynn and Jerry near the main gate appearing they had been there the whole time. Mary wondered if they had seen anything interesting. Jerry said just a whole lot of waiting around. Mary told them about meeting Dan Hoops the TV reporter and that he had asked them to come out the next morning to the Mausoleum giving them a chance to see Elvis's final resting spot. Mary suggested if they were interested she was sure Hoops would welcome them as well. The possibility excited both. Roger informed them he and Mary were on their way back to the hotel and then out to discover a little more of Memphis if they would like to join them. Mary was pleasantly surprised when they said they were ready for a change and that sounded good.

On the way, back to the hotel, Lynn said they had met some interesting people at Graceland. Mary asked Lynn if he had been playing the music box. Lynn smiled and told her the box did seem to have an appeal. Mary wondered where the people were from they had met. Lynn said you could name it North Carolina, Illinois, Kentucky basically from all over. Mary had to ask if there was any talk about the hoax theory. Jerry said no, but there were a few who claimed they had seen Elvis in the Mansion probably the same man they had seen the night before and then added people want attention that's all. Lynn commented on how crazy the day had been.

Once back at the hotel, it was apparent it mattered little what time you entered the lobby it was always busy. Those in training were getting an accelerated course on the ins and outs of running a hotel. One could say they were getting the equivalent of a Master's Degree in Hotel Operations. This week everyone worked.

The plan was for them to grab a shower and change before going back out. Once in the room, Mary decided to give Charles a call. Luckily, he was still in the office. She sensed he was glad to hear from her and she assured him everything was fine and she had much to report and told him about some of the rumors. Charles was intrigued by the notion that Elvis may have staged his death. But believed it to be too farfetched, but he looked forward to hearing more about it. Mary thanked him once again for believing in her. Telling him; "I've learned so much this experience will make me a better reporter." Charles said he never questioned her skills or desire and he was happy to hear the assignment was going well. Mary said she would see him Friday. Charles once again told her to be careful, and he looked forward to talking with her then.

MAMA'S MONEY

It wasn't long before everyone was back in the lobby looking forward to their night out. They decided to try the club Hoops had recommended Mama's Money. The club was close to the previous night spot The Music Barn. The popularity of the club was evident by a crowded parking lot. Though it looked as if they may have a wait Roger was able to cash in on his accent for a quick entrance. After hearing, Roger asks how long a wait it would be. The perky brunette at the door asked Roger if that was a true accent. He assured her it was his true tongue but was trying to learn the Memphis slang. She smiled and told him; "that's where I can help you." Roger just smiled and reaffirmed it would be quite an undertaking. The rest of the group remained silent figuring it was best to let Roger do the talking. The brunette then asked Roger how many were in his party. Roger blushed, a little and said just the four of us unless you care to join us. This bit of flirting sealed the deal as she led us into the club even helping them find a table.

Once again disco seemed to be the music of choice, and polyester ruled the fashion scene. Mama's Money was a rather modern club, wardrobe aside the club did provide a pleasant change from the day's activities. The song "*Don't leave me this away*" by Thelma Huston was playing when the waitress arrived. The song seemed rather appropriate considering the week's events. It was pure disco, but the lyrics rang true after all it was the night before Elvis would truly leave the building.

The popularity of disco music had become phenomenal in the last few years. Using an orchestrated sound that relied on magnified instrumentation the sound was different from traditional rock n roll. Hoops must have enjoyed the sound since the club was his recommendation. The over produce sound had hit a cord with the public Mary was yet to become a convert. Tonight's crowd was little different from the one at the Music Barn a fair mix of locals and tourist. Mama's Money was defiantly the place to forget the funeral and enjoy some dancing.

It didn't take Mary long to find out one can never truly leave a story. They had only been seated for a short time when a commotion broke out at the entrance. The subject of the uproar was the arrival of James Brown. James Brown *Soul Brother Number 1* was creating quite a scene as he and his entourage made their way into the club. It looked as if Brown was holding court, moving about the room talking to the patrons. Mary told Roger she hated to be the one to break it to him, but it looked like the *God Father of Soul* had replaced his English charm.

Mary was curious to what Brown was saying to everyone. She ventured over to where he was speaking, and there she overheard him telling those listening how much he loved Elvis. Brown said he and Elvis enjoyed a deep friendship with mutual admiration. Brown was the ultimate self-promoter and entertainer as he spoke of Elvis he was still promoting his career. Though James Brown was a music legend, his popularity was not what it used to be. Disco music seemed to be the avenue for a different kind of artist leaving the standard barriers of rock n roll behind. James Brown had been given several monikers during his career, everything from *Soul Brother No. 1 to Sex Machine*. Even as he paid tribute to a dear friend, he was enjoying the limelight. He told one patron he had just returned from the mansion, where he asked Vernon for a few minutes alone with the King. Brown said he told Vernon he loved Elvis immensely saying Elvis had the ability to reach across the lines of society with his soulful sound; everyone loved Elvis black and white. He brought people together with a unique sound. Brown credited Elvis for helping open many a door for black entertainers by demonstrating a love for the soulful black sound. He said he would always be grateful for what Elvis did for him and the music industry.

Brown had a clever self-promotional routine if anyone asked for an autograph a member of his entourage would pull out a glossy photo of Brown already signed. It was interesting to learn Brown had already signed the pictures and had added a song title added. One said Papa's Got a Brand-New Bag, James Brown. Another had the title I Got the Feelin, James Brown. You had to love the way Brown operated. One of his many monikers billed him as the hardest working man is show business and tonight was no exception.

When Mary returned to the table empty handed, Roger questioned her luck with the soul man. Mary told him not to worry the night was young. Roger acknowledged Brown was a huge star in London, suggesting the Brit's tend to hold on to the old while embracing the new. Soon Brown was making his way around the club pausing briefly at various tables to do one of his patent dance steps. Everyone agreed that the man had the moves. Brown finally approached their table. Surely, he was intrigued with Lynn and his jam box. After reaching the table, Brown looked to Lynn smiled and wondered what song was playing. As if on cue Lynn quickly turns the volume up and plays Chapel of Love. James Brown immediately started singing along as Lynn and Jerry join in. When the song ended, James looked at Lynn and told him; he liked his style.

Lynn introduced himself as the leader of Elvis's black fan club in New York City. James quickly did one of his screams followed by a laugh. Brown spotted Mary and asked if she was a member of the Godfather of Souls Fan Club. Mary didn't miss a beat telling him she was indeed. Before saying anything else, one of Brown's entourage pulled out a signed picture and gave it to her. It was signed James Brown Say It Loud I'm Black, and I'm Proud. She thanked him for the photo and immediately asked him if he minded if she asked him a few questions. Before he could answer Mary introduced herself telling him, she was a reporter for a small-town paper in Georgia. She felt this information would help considering Brown's home was Augusta Georgia. Brown then said he always had time for a pretty face especially one from home. He asked where home was for her. Telling him Dublin, Brown smiled and stated he had played there many times adding it's a nice community.

Mary asked if Brown could talk about Elvis and the death. Brown seemed very genuine as he said;

"The world has lost not only a righteous singer but also a good man. Our friendship dates back several years; he was the first white soul brother and boy did he have the soul."

Mary asked his thought on the fans Elvis left behind how would, they be affected.

"He's gone in the physical sense, but his music will live on for eternity. His death is a sad reminder that death is part of life, But Elvis had left us so many powerful songs and memories to cherish."

Before leaving the table, everyone received a signed photo. Walking away, Brown told the group to keep the faith and remember the Presley family in their prayers.

Roger couldn't resist asking Lynn if James Brown's music could replace Elvis. Lynn laughed and just said how cool it was to meet James Brown. Jerry said it's not every day you get to harmonize with someone like James Brown. As everyone admired, their signed photo's Lynn said he might just have to branch out a bit. Seeing Lynn this animated surprised Mary, he was either becoming more comfortable with the group or had been enjoying a few too many beers.

Brown's presence had brought everyone back to the death. Mary decided now was as good of time as any to get Lynn's take on it all. She hoped to take advantage of Lynn's talkative mood. Mary wondered how Lynn had become such a big fan. Lynn placed his photo of Brown on the table telling her it was the music, Mary somewhat skeptical repeated the music.

"Yea the music; all kidding aside the first time I heard him I was impressed with his voice and his soul. The man could entertain, and I loved it. From his movement to his sound Elvis offered something for everyone; his talent crossed ethnic and racial lines appealing to all cultures. I think more blacks would have appreciated the music if they just let go of the notion a white man was stealing the black man's culture. Elvis had soul no matter his color, and once I realized it, my appreciation just grew. I may feel a little outnumbered, but I know Elvis welcomed everyone black white rich poor that was the man."

Mary knew the rumors surrounding the death bothered Lynn earlier he said he didn't like the way he felt when hearing them. Lynn was a fan and felt the rumors only invited criticism not support.

Lynn asked Mary about the rumors wondering if she felt there could be any truth to them. Mary said she didn't know what to make of it, but it did make for good conversation. She felt people were going to believe what they want to believe. She then sighed;

"there are more than a few Americans who claimed we never landed on the moon. Saying it was all filmed in Arizona. So, I don't know what to believe when it comes to death I just write the obituary column, I don't verify them. But I've got to believe that Elvis is dead even if the corpse didn't look real."

Roger was listening in and added he didn't know much about funerals but he felt if Elvis were alive the funeral and news would have been handled differently. Roger went on saying consider if all this is fake, Elvis could easily be upstairs at Graceland watching the whole thing, and that would be a bit creepy for everyone. Lynn said it would be more than creepy it would be plain disturbing, adding he didn't want to talk about it anymore. Soon Jerry asked Mary if she would like to dance. The DJ had ventured away from disco and was now playing *You Ain't Seen Nothing* Yet by Bachman-Turner Overdrive. Mary took his hand, and they were soon on the dance floor.

Jerry and Mary stopped dancing when the DJ began playing a tribute to Elvis the first song was Suspicious Minds, telling everyone it was Elvis's last number one. As Suspicious Minds played, they returned to the table where Lynn and Roger were discussing the song.

Lynn told Roger; "I was 15 at the time and it was the first Elvis record I ever bought. I brought it home, and my parents nearly freaked. Wondering why I was spending my money on a white man? I think they would have been happier if I was buying the Temptations or the Four Tops. Not some over-hyped white boy as they liked to call him."

Mary laughed saying; "If it was any consolation I was buying the Four Tops and Jerry Butler, and my parents questioned my taste as well. I loved the Motown sound."

Lynn added he liked Motown, but it was Elvis he made a connection.

Before the song ended, Lynn and Jerry had started to sing along. Jerry laughingly told Lynn he could have a future if only he could sing. Lynn smiled and asked Jerry how his singing career was working out?

Mary was surprised by the question, and she wondered if Jerry was a singer or was this an inside joke. After all, he told her he was a plumber. Jerry in a rather satirical tone said; "plumbing pays the bills singing entertains the ladies." Mary learned that Jerry did do some singing on the side at small clubs in the city. But for Jerry, there was more money in broken pipes than there was with his singing pipes. Roger in a callous fashion told him his competition was down one singer. Jerry laughed and then said he had been thinking about something and would like their input.

"I've been given some thought to putting together an Elvis tribute band, creating an impression of the king while singing his songs."

Lynn joked with Jerry and said maybe even love some of his women. Jerry smiled and said that was an idea he could get behind. He then became serious telling the group;

"I know most of the songs and have seen him perform enough that I could copy some of Elvis's patented moves. An act dedicated to the memory of Elvis."

Mary told him it didn't hurt to dream. Roger said you might want to hit the buffet table for about three months before you take on that venture. Though they were all laughing at the prospect, Jerry had a look suggesting he was considering such a venture. Lynn quickly informed him that he had taken a lot of grief being a black Elvis fan and Elvis was worth it, he wasn't sure a skinny white kid from the Bronx's would be worth it. Jerry smiled and said he was just thinking out loud.

The mood of the club was very upbeat everyone was having a good time. Roger decided to branch out and try to find someone who wanted to dance. Soon Roger and a reporter from the Associated Press, whom Mary had met earlier, were on the dance floor and Jerry and Mary decide to join them. Lynn remained at the table with his jam box. Mary then asked Jerry if Lynn ever went anywhere without the box? Jerry just smiled. Mary then added; "they were probably lucky it wasn't an eight-track."

As everyone gathered back at the table, Roger said he learned Caroline Kennedy was at the Mansion earlier in the evening. Supposedly Kennedy was interviewing mourners outside the mansion when Vernon, Presley's father asked if she would like to come inside. Jerry immediately said Damn he wished he had seen her she was an Elvis fan he would like to get to know. Lynn looked at him saying "I quote Mary it doesn't hurt to dream."

Roger said;

"Supposedly Caroline and her family were watching the national coverage when she decided to come to Memphis to get the story first hand. I think she is doing work for the New Yorker. Word is Ms. Kennedy was very complimentary to the family telling Vernon that Elvis made more than the music he created hope and optimism. He had the ability to entertain and bring people together creating joy and love."

This acclamation just made Jerry and Lynn smile. Mary told Roger the Kennedy's were probably the closest thing the states had to a royal family they were uniformly loved.

The Hustle by Van McCoy began to play, and Mary turned to Roger telling him she wanted to dance. Though it was getting late, the club was still busy. Once on the dance floor, Mary noticed Matt Saunders with a group of his friends. Catching his eye, she waved. As she and Roger finished dancing Saunders came over to her saying they needed to quit meeting like this. Mary smiled saying it must be faith and then wondered if the rumor mill had cranked out any more stories.

"It continues to get stranger and stranger. The latest one is someone purchased a one-way ticket to Buenos Aeries less than two hours after news of the death broke. But what makes this interesting is John Burros purchased the ticket."

"So, who is John Burros and why does it matter?"

Laughing Saunders says; "few knew it but John Burros happened to be one of the alias's Elvis used when traveling. Mr. John Burros was his special handle, and now Mr. Burros is on his way to Buenos Aeries. I also learned that Elvis did no prep work for his tour, a tour that should have started today. It's almost like Elvis knew he wouldn't be touring."

Mary said; "It still sounds questionable at best maybe you should consider the possibility of suicide." Saunders said he just reports the rumors who knows what the truth is. Mary acknowledged the rumors did keep things interesting and had the makings of one hell of a story.

Saunders said;

"I could buy the suicide theory easier than the hoax if the corpse didn't appear to be wax. Maybe the mortician was off his game, but the corpse sure left a lot of folks with questions. And unfortunately, many of those questions were (what or who was that in the casket). Let's hope all this speculation is the result of an overly emotional public. But in my business, I'm always trying to look behind the curtain."

Roger said if he were a betting man he'd bet Elvis was dead but it certainly could have been handled better, maybe they shouldn't have been in such a race to get him buried. Everyone agreed if the death was a hoax they certainly would have come up with a better story than having him die on his throne.

Mary wanted to know if Saunders felt there would be any interest in tribute band or impersonators when it came to Elvis and his music. She asked him if he had seen the guy in the blue Elvis shirt. Matt pointed out there were about five guys in the club wearing blue Elvis shirts. Saunders said you mean the one you at your table. Mary smiled and said;

"Yes, that's the one. He's a Plummer from New York and is considering becoming an Elvis impersonator. He believes with Elvis dying there will be a market for tribute acts. He doesn't even feel talent's that important just show respect and honor the man, and the fans will forgive the lack of talent."

Saunders felt it was a reasonable idea.

"Elvis has plenty of fans who are holding on to anything they can, so why not a skinny Plummer from New York singing Rock a Hula and Jail House Rock. I like the concept of an Elvis impersonator, and just think if Elvis did fake his death then he could come back as the ultimate impersonator. And then he wouldn't have to live under the same microscope he has been under for the last ten years."

Mary just responded he was unbelievable. They both laughed, and Saunders assured her that soon all the speculation would only be a memory.

While they were laughing about all the theories and rumors, a young man Saunders knew came to their table he seemed obviously shaken and wanted to talk with Saunders. Saunders greeted the man a friend named Don Bradford. Not only was Bradford shook up it was evident he had been drinking. He then told Saunders something terrible had happened. Silence soon replaced the laughter at the table. With everyone's attention Bradford began to speak. The young man began to tell a story of a tragedy he witnessed earlier at Graceland.

Saunders broke the silence asking what had happened. Bradford looked disturbed as he told everyone some drunken kid crashed his car into a group of mourners. Bradford had everyone's attention. Judging from Bradford's tone, it wasn't necessary to ask. But Mary did anyway wanting to know if anyone was hurt.

"Yea it was bad some drunk guy not much older than a kid drove his car directly into the crowd. This guy just drives right into the crowd, and he hits three young girls two of which I know are dead the other I'm not sure she was taken away by ambulance."

The news stunned Mary she repeated his words "he drove into the crowd." Bradford confirmed the man had driven into the mourners and then tried to speed away. He kept driving with one of the girls still trapped by his car. Shaking his head, Bradford said; "it was awful no one should die that way, and for that matter, no one should have to witness such a tragedy."

Saunders wondered if they caught the driver. Bradford said;

"The police had to chase the guy down, he was so drunk I don't think he realized what he had done. As the police were pulling him from the car beer cans began rolling into the street, and the crowds began yelling kill him kill him."

Mary asked if others were hurt. Bradford thought it was just the girls again adding how terrible, it was,

"The guy was swerving all over the place it was a wonder more weren't killed. The girls were talking to a policeman when hit. Innocently standing there and some fool mow's them down. The cop jumped out of the way, but the girls didn't have a chance."

Saunders asked if Bradford knew anything about the girls. Bradford said;

"They looked to be teenagers just taking part in the candlelight vigil. It happened so fast they probably didn't know what hit them."

The news sucked the air out of the room. The death of Elvis was a sad occasion, but this horrible accident was an unnecessary tragedy quickly changing the mood of everyone.

This news put a new light on the events of the day sadness, not felt before had fallen over the group. Anyone of them could have been a victim, of such a senseless tragedy. Everyone was stunned no one knew what to say. The story began to circulate the club with the number of victims varying from 2-5. But Bradford assured everyone it was three, and at that time two were dead. Mary thought of the young girls all close to her age. She couldn't help but cry. She didn't know the victims but could identify with them and why they were at the mansion. Everyone at Graceland had a reason to be there, and no one should've been hurt much less killed. Mary assumed they were there to demonstrate their love for Elvis. Now gone, she feared their lives would only become a footnote to the funeral. They deserve more; Mary began to wonder how she could pay tribute to their memory.

All remained silent as Bradford left the table. Mary wondered if the tragedy would have any impact on Elvis's legacy. Saunders said;

"For one thing, these deaths should affect the hoax theory. If Elvis did orchestrate a charade and he is still living this tragedy would most likely prevent him from every returning to the stage. None of this would have happened if there were no funeral or candle light vigil."

Mary wondered; "Are you saying Elvis's death could partially be responsible for these deaths? I don't feel it's fair to blame Elvis."

Saunders agreed;

"It may not be fair, but earlier today it might have been an innocent charade, but now it's a tragic story. The death of the girls may prevent anyone from ever knowing the truth. If Elvis were participating in a hoax, it would be hard to imagine the guilt he must be feeling. How could he ever return to the stage with such guilt associated with these deaths."

Mary was silent as she wiped her tears thinking of the young girls and how their lives had been cut short and for what? Roger asked if she was okay. Mary told him;

"The deaths bother me, and I am having some difficulty with the news. Those girls were just paying their respect, and now they're dead. The vigil will continue, and the funeral will take place. Few will know the girls came to Memphis much less died here. The whole thing makes me nauseates. It was a senseless tragedy, and that's what bothers me the most."

Mary began to realize the story she was looking for was not only the grief of fans but the accompanying tragedy. Anyone could report on the funeral, but she needed to tell the story of the people. The funeral was only a small part of the story. Mary needed to tell of the emotions and the tears that thousands shared at the candlelight vigil as well as the funeral. The real story was with those who came together from all over the world and what they encountered and now their experience including the tragic deaths. She should write about those who came and why. What were the fans hoping to find or say by being in Memphis? To Mary, this was the story. She had sold Charles of the idea of covering the funeral with a personal touch and now she could. These deaths of the girls had made it personal. Why would so many sacrifices so much, to say good-bye to a fallen rock star? People spending time and money, to pay homage to a man they only knew through his career. And now two girls and possibly a third had given their lives trying to say good-bye.

The question facing Mary was what motivates people to come together for such an event hoping to honor someone they never really knew. Thousands were lining the streets of Graceland demonstrating their love for a celebrity persona. And now you could add in a disregard for personal safety. Mary wondered what these actions say about society. Even if those surrounding Graceland felt they knew Elvis, did they know him or just know a marketed image. Were the mourners searching for an identity? An identity wrapped up in a flawed entertainer. Did anybody deserve this kind of devotion much less an entertainer? This tragedy was senseless and should never have happened.

Maybe it was her emotions or the lack of sleep, but Mary was now questioning everything especially the worship some held for entertainers. She compared the unrealistic worship of the fans to something resembling a cult, where people have a need to believe in something or somebody. And this week Elvis fit the bill. Mary wondered if society admired the man or the image. Being thankful and respectful of one's talent was admirable, but Mary feared what she was witnessing at Graceland was over the top and unhealthy.

Elvis paid the price for the love and the devotion of his fans. Elvis lived under the pressure of his fans demands and their expectations, costing him his freedom. He couldn't live a normal life everything he did or attempted to do, was on display for public praise or ridicule. A tough order for any man.

Mary also wondered why the public would have such love for a man who was battling his set of demons, demons that most likely contributed to his early death. Society could put undue pressure on its hero's often refusing to see the negatives thus allowing for self-destruction as an adoring public looked on.

Mary began talking to Roger about her feelings. He once again was a stable influence telling her she needed to separate things out;

"The death of the young girls is certainly a tragedy but remember these girls were doing what they wanted."

Mary responded; "they weren't looking to die." Roger told her,

"That's not what I'm saying. It was a tragedy, but remember the girls were experiencing life and there are no guarantees when it comes to life or death."

Mary knew the girls were living their lives, but she questioned why they were there in the first place. She felt if all the negative reports of Elvis were true why would so many demonstrate such love. Roger reminded her; "That's up to the fans, not you or me."

Mary felt blind loyalty contributed to the death of these innocent girls, and that's what bothered her. She added;

"Something else is bothering me. How will others remember these girls? I'm afraid their deaths will only be an afterthought. These girls had families and loved ones, but few would give them any thought because of the commotion and events surrounding Elvis's death. There will be no candlelight vigil or flower lined streets honoring their memory, but their deaths are just as tragic as that of Elvis if not more so."

Roger agreed; "You'll get no argument from me. But remember you can't change history, but you can report it."

Mary knew she was tired, and her emotions were getting the best of her. Roger told her she had a right to be upset everyone should be it was a tragedy, but she couldn't allow the tragedy to cloud her perspective or her reporting.

Mary knew it wasn't fair, but if Elvis turns out to be alive and all of this is a hoax, then he should bear some of the responsibility for the deaths. She felt one can't live on the public stage and not realize your actions have consequences a celebrity lifestyle does come with some responsibility to the fans.

Roger injected; "It seems that everyone has a need to belong to something it's what makes us who we are. That's just life. Did you ever belong to a sorority in college?"

"I did why?"

"Sororities, fraternities, clubs whatever you call them represented people wanting to belong and share a common goal. The thousands of fans who are here in Memphis for the funeral all wanted to belong to something, and a tribute to Elvis was where they gravitated. Coming to Memphis allowed these fans to share a love for Elvis and a common purpose, that of honoring the man. Last week Jerry was a plumber and Lynn a mechanic both sharing an appreciation for the music of Elvis Presley; their love for the music and the man brought them to Memphis, and here they found a much larger group with the same beliefs. All those on the street or who filed by the casket had a similar reason. Consider it this way the crowd can resemble a mass of humanity brought together by a single event. And those fans that came are now finding comfort her in Memphis."

Mary began to consider Rogers thoughts maybe the outpouring of emotions said something about society and the need people have for each other. She knew that the mourners all had an appreciation for Elvis. Maybe those gathering in Memphis failed to see the controversies only seeing the man, a man who didn't protest the war but gladly served his country, a man who lived on a public stage but never used the stage to disrupt and the man who shared his talent for all to enjoy.

Roger added that once the fans came together in Memphis, they realized others shared their love for Elvis making the attraction even greater. He told Mary not to be so critical of the few days the mourners would spend together they were there to find comfort in others on Elvis Presley Boulevard. The few days they spend together mourning Elvis's passing, is a small price to pay for the love and joy he brought them. Next week they will return to their jobs and families the flowers will be gone, and the streets will be empty. Roger told Mary he likes to consider the funeral and the mourning a celebration of the human spirit. Mary agreed and thanked him for his perspective realizing the funeral was a good reflection on society.

Once Lynn and Jerry learned of the accident they like everyone else was shocked by the news of the deaths. Lynn wondered how life could be so cruel; noting that all they wanted to do was show their love for Elvis. Lynn went on to say this was a tragedy that never should have happened. Mary knew the news had affected her view of everything but was now wondering how this horrific event affected Lynn. Lynn acknowledged it was a terrible thing, adding that it just adds to his frustration and anger about the death. He knew you couldn't blame someone for dying, but if Elvis's death was self-inflicted or turned out to be a hoax, he wasn't sure he could ever forgive him. Lynn added if it comes out that the death is anything but natural then Elvis has done a great miss-service to the thousands who supported him throughout his career. Mary told him she feared the deaths of these young girls would go unnoticed not receiving the attention they deserve after all they had families that love them and will miss them. Jerry said you know Elvis would never have wanted such a horrible thing to happen; you can't blame him for the tragedy of others he wanted people to live and enjoy life. Mary then added that might be true, but it doesn't lessen the anger for such senseless deaths.

Jerry didn't want to blame Elvis for the actions of others, but Lynn was disappointed and frustrated with it all. Each knew that the deaths would not have occurred if Elvis were still alive, there would be no need for a candlelight vigil. The rumors and innuendo that Elvis may still be alive added to Lynn's frustration. Jerry tried to assure Lynn Elvis was dead and he couldn't blame the man for dying and was sure Elvis would have preferred the other option. Lynn said considering what they had learned he wasn't so sure adding if only Elvis cared about himself as much as his fans did for him, maybe he would be here today. Jerry said; "Sadly it may have just been his time and it could have also been those girls time." Lynn felt Jerry was simplifying a tragedy that should have never occurred.

The way both men were processing Elvis's death and those of the young girls interested Mary. Lynn who had worshiped the man was now questioning his emotions. Mary wasn't sure who he was angry with, himself for being such a devoted fan or with Elvis for dying. Roger shared; sometimes people find identity in others, and maybe Lynn was discovering he didn't care for this identity. Jerry seemed to negate any criticism almost as if he was assuming a role of caretaker. Jerry wanted the legacy of Elvis to go on and not be tarnished by these deaths or by information that would bring embarrassment to the man or his family.

Mary's interest in the hoax theory, and now the deaths of the young girls only added to her curiosity. She wanted to talk with Saunders more about how these deaths would impact a hoax.

Saunders felt; "These tragic deaths change everything if Elvis did fake his death hoping to get some time away from the stress of being a star, the girl's deaths would prevent him from ever returning to the public stage. No matter how you feel about Elvis; I don't feel he could ever handle the criticism that would come with the unveiling of such a hoax. The funeral endangered many lives and contributed to the actual death of some. If Elvis had not staged his death, these fans would still be alive, and that is a heavy burden to bear, especially heavy for a man so dependent on his fans. If Elvis is still alive, I don't feel anyone will ever see him in the same light again."

Mary knew if he did return he would have a lot of explaining to do addressing his strange behavior and now the death of innocent fans. It was a compelling story and was making her look at everything differently.

Roger made one more trip to the dance floor, only to return to the table ready to leave. He told Mary he needed to get him out of there. He wasn't sure he could take any more dancing or grieving Elvis fans. Mary knew he had been talking to a redhead reporter again and wondered if he finished with his interview. Roger smiled and said he was, and hopefully; she with him. Both laughed and were ready to leave. Lynn and Jerry were also ready to go, and for the first time, Mary noticed Lynn was not playing any music she even asked if he needed batteries. Lynn surprised her with his response;

"I'm thinking of letting the man go. The death of the girls has caused me to think, and I'm not happy with my thoughts. It seems to me I came to Memphis, to honor a man who let himself and his fans down."

Back at the hotel, there was no talk of the deaths. The Shriners were active making it difficult to tell if they were starting or ending a party. The Shriners did love to party. A mini car was now parked close to the front desk. How it got there a mystery, and its removal would be an even bigger challenge.

The four of them agreed to regroup in a couple of hours to go out to the Mausoleum and meet up with Hoops. Roger and Mary took the elevator, and Lynn and Jerry decided to visit the hotel bar one more time. Lynn was dealing with a lot of emotions and maybe felt a drink was in order.

In the elevator, Mary explained to Roger; "I'm not sure what I've gotten myself into; the story may be over my head."

Roger told her; "We only get over our heads when we have to create a story, and this story certainly needs no creation."

"I just fear all the twist and turns not knowing which direction to take."

"Don't worry once you begin writing, your report, the story will lead you, and all those twist and turns will serve as a roadmap for your article. You will do a fine job just follows your intuition?"

When the doors to the elevator opened, Roger told her not to worry, to get some sleep knowing the final chapter was yet to come.

Mary was so tired once she reached her room she had a difficult time falling asleep. She grabbed her pen and pad and began jotting down notes from the day. She constructed a list of the rumors she had heard, plus she listed the names of the dignitaries that had been seen or were reportedly coming to the funeral.

A NEW DAY

After sleeping only, a couple of hours Mary awoke to realize her time in Memphis would soon be ending, and she needed to get busy. She had to shift her approach from gathering information to writing the story; after all, she had a deadline to meet. Her challenge was in the direction she would choose constructing and reporting on the story.

Hoping a shower would wake her Mary took her time seeking energy from the flowing water? Her final day in Memphis had arrived. Once dressed Mary made her way to the lobby, she wasn't the only one dragging none of the others had made it down. In the grill, Mary got a cup of coffee and ordered wheat toast and bacon. The grill had remained open the entire time. Mary felt this was a good description of her stay in Memphis open 24 hours. Soon the funeral would be history, and she and Memphis could begin to return to some semblance of normalcy.

It wasn't long before Roger joined her. Mary knew though only together for a short while they had already spent some quality time with each other. Once again, he would try the coffee from Mary's point of view it was the only thing that had not gone his way.

Shortly Lynn and Jerry appeared. Lynn carried the jam box, but it wasn't resting on his shoulder or playing. Of the two Jerry seemed more excited about the day. The last day would supply more memories though Mary knew she already had enough memories to last for years.

The schedule for the day included a visit to Forest Hills in the morning then return to Graceland for the funeral. If time allowed following the funeral, they would return to Forest Hills to see the interment. Roger would then drop everyone off at the airport. It was going to be a busy but exciting day. Roger was the only one not checking out, opting to leave for Nashville the next day. Everyone else had brought down their luggage and were preparing to leave.

Forest Hills Cemetery was a short distance from Graceland. A small crowd was already gathering on the street. Several TV stations were doing lived feeds from the grounds. Many of the flowers had been moved from Graceland and were now reaching across the drive and covering most of the grassy entrance. Fortunately, Hoops saw Mary and Roger almost immediately. Hoops told one of the security guards to allow them through the ropes. Once they caught up with him, Mary introduced Lynn and Jerry hoping he didn't mind her inviting a few friends. Hoops said;

"Not at all, the more, the better. It'll be a few minutes before taping." He then offered to show everyone around. He leads them to a plot heavily decorated with flowers located about 300 feet from the mausoleum. It was the burial spot of Elvis's mother, Gladys Presley. Hoops said he felt Presley's mother would eventually be moved to one of the four spots available in the mausoleum adding he thought Vernon and his current wife would use the other spots once the need arose. Hoops soon said he needed to get to work asking the group to stand nearby and they would be seen in the background, giving that personal feel.

While Hoops was filing his report, Mary studied the grave site of Gladys Presley. The modest marker surprised her mostly considering how ornate Graceland was. Once Hoops had finished his segment, he came over to Mary; asking if it was what she was expecting. "Not at all, I guess I felt it would be more ornate and marked differently."

Hoops said;

"Personally, I feel the grave is simple by design. Elvis would visit his mother's grave regularly, and its simplicity helped keep those moments personal and private. Elvis would wear disguises to avoid public recognition seeking some private time with his mother. No matter your thoughts of Elvis he was devoted to his mother in life and death. When Gladys was, alive Elvis looked to her for love and guidance she was a good mother. Things might have turned out differently if she had lived longer."

Mary questioned how she died.

"It was a heart attack happened when Elvis was in the Army, Vernon and Gladys were living in Graceland at the time. Supposedly, Elvis wanted her funeral to be held at Graceland, but was convinced by his agent Colonel Parker, to have it at the funeral home."

"Why what difference would it make."

"Parker was worried about security. But she did lie in state at Graceland for two days."

Mary was surprised with the two days that was longer than the time they were giving Elvis. Feeling it was strange, they gave two days to a woman few knew and only a couple of hours for the king of rock n roll. Hoops agreed it was strange how they rushed to bury Elvis yet took days to bury his mother. Hoops said it was his understanding Vernon was so upset he had a hard time burying her. Elvis finally convinced him to have the funeral. Mary noticed that Presley's mother had died on August 14th creepily close to the same day Elvis died. Mary thought that the story continued to take bizarre twist and turns and wondered where it would all end.

As they began walking away from the gravesite, Mary asked Hoops about the deaths of the young girls. Hoops said it was a senseless tragedy and reported the third girl had died as well. Mary just shook her head. She asked if there was any other information regarding the accident. Hoops said he understood it was a freak accident caused by a deranged drunk driver. The young girls were taking part in a candlelight vigil and had crossed the highway to ask a police officer something and while talking with the officer a car passed by the crowd and then turned around and came back at a high rate of speed striking and killing the young ladies. Surprisingly the officer wasn't hurt he got out of the way. Mary thought just how awful this was. She told Hoops;

"I'm glad I wasn't there that's something I never hope to witness. Do you know how the crowd reacted?"

"The story only gets worse the driver kept going after hitting the girls. Once the car came to a stop, he began to run away on foot. Everyone was stunned. "I'm sure I will be covering the story over the next few days."

Mary took a moment and then said;

"What bothered me is how three innocent girls died honoring Elvis; they had loved ones they had lives, and yet they will hardly be mentioned in the coverage."

"Well, Mary that will be up to us we need to share the young girl's stories. If we don't do it who will?"

Hoops took the opportunity to interview Mary and Roger asking a few questions. It was the standard line of questioning wanting to know where they were from and how the death had impacted them. He made no mention they were with the press, giving the illusion that they had come just to pay their respects. When finished, Mary said she hoped Tammy didn't see the report she'll think Hoops had short term memory loss. Hoops laughed and told Mary Tammy knew it was the story not necessarily the facts that create viewers. Mary asked if they would see him at the mansion. Hoops said; He hoped to be there before the procession starts. He suggested they try to camp out near the entrance reiterating it was going to be a small funeral and the mansion couldn't accommodate many.

Once they finished with Hoops, Roger told Mary she might have a future on television she was quite polished with the interview. Both laughed at the notion they were going to be on television across the airways of Memphis. Mary was going to miss Roger and the friendship they had forged.

Back in the car, Lynn asked Mary if there was any more information about the young girls killed. After hearing Mary's account, he just stared out the window in silence. Mary knew everyone handles tragedies differently and this one was particularly bothering Lynn. Soon Lynn spoke saying he blamed the drunk driver, but everyone had a hand in this tragedy. Mary wondered what he meant. Lynn felt none of this would have ever occurred if the public had let the man die in peace. The Presley's should have been able to mourn in peace without all the distractions. Going on to say it's hard to imagine what the Presley family must be feeling innocent girls lose their life while honoring Elvis, it's so disturbing.

THE FUNERAL

At the mansion, everyone was staking out an advantage point to view the funeral. Waiting for what; a car and a procession, the sight was surreal. Mary felt the crowd was more sedate not showing as much emotion. It may have been a result of time or possibly the accident involving the young girls. The deaths had people thinking. Mary had an opportunity to speak with an eyewitness to the accident. She was in her early 30's and told Mary, she had been at the mansion for the last 24 hours and had not slept and had seen it all. She confirmed the reports of the two girls dying instantly and the third taken to the hospital. Telling Mary, it was awful and very disturbing; she felt it took the paramedics forever to get there, so the bodies just laid there on the street covered with blood everyone was in shock. Everybody was just so angry that such a violent act had taken place and innocent people losing their lives so meaninglessly. The driver had turned a special time into a tragic time, and it just wasn't fair.

Roger and Mary selected a place to stand that allowed them to view the outside grounds as well as the main entrance; Lynn and Jerry continued walking around not wanting to settle on a spot until they had too. Lynn seemed more distracted feeling the emotions of the tragedy as well as the funeral.

Mary learned that Ann Margaret and Dianne Cannon both former co-stars with Elvis would be in attendance this news appeared to excite Roger. Mary found it funny that after all Roger had witnessed and covered in his career, he was excited about the possibility of seeing these two actresses. She couldn't say much hoping to get a glimpse of former Memphis resident and actor George Hamilton who was rumored to be attending. The crowd began showing greater energy once the guessing game of who was arriving as the limos pulled into Graceland.

No one was certain who would attend it was all speculation. There was no guessing when James Brown arrived. He took the opportunity to walk through the crowd thanking everyone for being there adding it was an honor to Elvis and his legacy. He remained the constant showman making a striking image as he shook hands with those reaching out for him telling everyone to keep the family in their prayers. He seemed sincere, but he was also a great showman.

More flower arrangements were being collected and transported to the cemetery. Mary wondered how they would find space for all the arrangements. No matter how many they moved, there would be plenty left behind.

It would be Mary's last opportunity to talk with some of the mourners, so she decided to interview a few and find out why they came to Memphis. A young girl near them said she had only been at the mansion for only a couple of hours but had not slept for what seemed like days. She and her mother started driving from Lubbock Texas once they heard the news. Lubbock Texas has their own claim to Rock N Roll history being the home and burial site of the legendary Buddy Holly. The girl told Mary that she was there because of her mother. Her mom was a big fan of Elvis and wanted to come. The mother then said she felt it was the right thing to do. Mary asked her if she was a fan of Buddy Holly. The lady said she was more than a fan she went to High School with him and knew him when he was playing the skating rinks and Drive Inns throughout Lubbock. The lady said Holly's funeral was a modest occasion and she always felt more should have been done to honor him. The daughter spoke up again telling Mary her Mom was a fan of music, but she did love Elvis. To which the mother laughed and said I did love the man. The daughter added the music of Elvis and Holly filled their house.

If Mary ever doubted Elvis was the King all it took was a quick look around and view the huge crowd. Only nobility would get this type of coverage and devotion. And soon it would be over, and the burial of the King would take place, and a new King would emerge, but for now Rock N Roll history was standing still as fans from all over the world came together giving this king a proper farewell.

Mary began to reflect on the last 48 hours; so much had happened she had experienced almost every type of emotion. For such a short time, it was an experience of a lifetime. One continuous ride of excitement from the moment she boarded a small plane in Dublin to now Mary had witnessed it all. Complete strangers were now good friends, and she had a story to tell. All things considered, it was a trip for the ages.

Shortly before the scheduled start time, the funeral party began to arrive in earnest. A sea of white Limo's made their way onto the grounds. Unfortunately, it was impossible to see who occupied the limos leaving the speculation to everyone's imagination. When 2:00 o'clock arrived the crowds became solemn. The emotional day was hitting home, many in the crowd kept checking their watches knowing that soon Elvis would truly be laid to rest. Some held camera's hoping for that final photo once the funeral procession exited the house.

Security guards continued to hand out water to combat the heat as few were willing to leave their chosen spots. Many of the older mourners sat down on the pavement or the curb giving way to exhaustion. The heat would not keep them from offering their final good-byes no one was leaving. Close to two hours after the funeral had begun it was over. Those in attendance began to emerge from the mansion preparing for the trip to Forest Hills. Several Memphis police officers were present on motorcycles and in cars. Most stationed outside the gate, but a few motorcycles were on the grounds organizing the final procession. Soon two motorcycle cops led the way out of the grounds on to Presley Blvd for the short trip to Forest Hills. The first car out was a silver Cadillac followed by the white hearse then numerous limos. Mary stopped counting the limos at 10. The Hearse was flanked by motorcycles as they turned up the road. Cameras began to click. Police officers stood at attention saluting as the hearse drove by them. The crowds stood in silence as tears fell. Mary felt it was an eerie sight one that seemed to last an eternity. No one spoke until a police officer politely asks the mourners to begin dispersing needing to clear the streets.

Hoops had secured press passes for Mary and Roger so they could get on the grounds at Forest Hills and have an opportunity to cover the activity at the Mausoleum. They hoped to beat the procession knowing it would move slowly through the streets of Memphis to the cemetery. Earlier they had scouted out a back road that hopefully would help them arrive before the procession.

The four of them were soon parking at the cemetery when the procession began to arrive. It was a few minutes before the family and friends began to exit the cars making the walk to the Mausoleum.

Roger got his glimpse of Ann Margaret; Mary saw George Hamilton and of course James Brown was also visible. Everyone remained silent; there was no doubt Elvis was the King of Rock N Roll, and this was his final appearance.

At Forest Hills, the service was rather short, and from their vantage point, no one could hear the proceedings. To many, it appeared the pastor read something from the bible and then spoke to the family. In a matter of minutes, it was over, and the family began to make their way back to the limos. Mary noticed Vernon Presley helping an elderly lady into the lead car; Roger told her the lady was probably Elvis's grandmother. Soon the funeral procession had exited the cemetery. It was now history taking less than 72 hours for Elvis to be pronounced dead and buried. The short time lapse made it even more difficult to accept the death.

The entire experience was coming to an end for everyone. Mary felt they had time for one more visit to Graceland and possibly grab something to eat before leaving for the airport. Lynn and Jerry's flight was for 8:11 and Marys flight shortly after at 8:37. It wouldn't be long before everyone would be going their separate ways and for Mary saying goodbye would be difficult. She had to accept her adventure was coming to an end. Roger would be able to see everyone off before returning to the hotel for some much-needed rest. Once done with his story in Nashville Roger would return to London. Mary wasn't sure how he would get it all done, but he was cool in his approach a quality she hoped to immolate in her career.

The hoax theory still played on Mary's mind. She decided to stop at a pay phone and give Saunders a call. She was fortunate enough to catch him at his office. With the limited time, he agreed to meet them for a quick bite before they left for the airport. Saunders suggested a restaurant near Graceland, Gary's Silver Spoon.

The last view of Graceland showed litter covering the grounds thousands of flowers and only a handful of mourners remained. Things appeared to be returning to normal. Gary's silver spoon was easy to locate. Once inside the restaurant, they found Saunders sitting alone at a table. Saunders rose from his seat and motioned Mary and the others over. Seated at a large oval table and with a toothy grin asked everyone their thoughts of the funeral. No one answered right away everyone was still processing the last few days. Mary just shook her head and said the better question is what he thought since he was the expert on all the rumors.

Saunders told them things continue to get interesting a hazard of his profession. He had learned the casket supposedly weight over 900 lbs. Lynn was the first to say that seems like a lot. Saunders said;

"Oh, yea that is quite an increase normally a casket weighs between 100 to 300 pounds. Maybe they buried him with his money."

Lynn had become silent with his thoughts but wondered how six poll bearers could handle such weight. Saunders said he wasn't sure how anyone could handle such weight and then adding to the suspensions told everyone he understood the casket had an air conditioner in it designed to keep the body cool.

"An air conditioner?" Mary asked why anyone would ever consider putting an air conditioner in a casket. Saunders said well you might want to if the body is a wax replica. Roger a little annoyed with all the theories said: "so are we back to the wax body theory." Saunders said he speculated a wax body may need to be cooled and would also explain the extra weight. No one had any facts to back up any of the rumors or anything to support a hoax, but that didn't keep others from spreading or being caught up in them.

Roger wondered if Saunders had any details of the funeral. Saunders told them they probably knew as much as he did but he proceeded to tell her that the service conducted by Rex Hubbard, a famed television evangelist. Hubbard was a friend of the family. Saunders also understood the music room was set up for the service and nearly 200 people attended. Jack Kahane a comedian who opened for Elvis on the road made some commits before the service. Mary remembered him opening the Mobile show she attended in June. Lynn and Jerry both commented they enjoyed him when they had seen him with Elvis. Saunders then told them, C. W. Bailey, a local pastor from Wooddale Church of Christ in Memphis did that the main eulogy. Mary felt the service helped demonstrate that it was a true funeral and Elvis was truly dead and the hoax theory was just crazy thinking. Saunders reminded her that if you are going to fake your death, you better make it seem as real as possible.

Before leaving Saunders gave Mary, another rumored. One as strange as any. He told her that some are saying Elvis who had been recognized by former President Nixon as a Drug Enforcement Officer was turning over some evidence that exposed a crime ring with Mafia ties and for this information, he was given a new identity and placed in the witness protection program. If this were the case, he would have had the backing of the government making it much easier and plausible for such a hoax to work. With the government's backing, he would finally find the peace and privacy he so much desired.

Mary felt witness protection for John Jones would be a lot easier than for someone as recognizable as Elvis. Jerry hearing this said Elvis was an entertainer and once the entertainment bug is in your system it would be hard just to walk away. Saunders just shook his head and added that no matter what the truth is everyone could count on the rumors living on and he was sure there were some more rumors to come. Saunders added it was just human nature and closed by saying no matter what one thinks it may be fair to say Elvis's career is over, but his legacy will live on for quite some time. Adding that people want to hold on to their beliefs and in doing so can create the image they wish to remember. Roger added that Elvis wouldn't be the first entertainer to receive a bounce from his death. Saunders held up his beer and toasted the story real or fiction it was a great story. He then said, "The King is Dead Long Live the King." Everyone held up their glasses and repeated the words Long Live the King.

Saunders had stoked the fires of doubt and made everyone look beyond the reported story Mary knew this could serve a journalist well. The last few days had certainly given everyone something to consider. Mary had enjoyed it all including the rumors. She had made new friends and received an education in human nature.

As Mary left the restaurant, she gave Saunders a hug and wished him well. Telling him if any rumors turned up true to give her a call. He assured her he would, but then said he had to lay Elvis to rest he had a pressing matter involving a suspecting housewife and cheating husband. Mary smiled and told him she knew he was the man for the job.

Walking to the car, Roger said it seemed Saunders might have won her over. Mary answered;

"I not sure what to make of all his theories but I have to admit I've enjoyed getting to know him. He seems to have an approach to the rumors giving them some credibility."

Roger responded; "the man did spin quite a tale."

Mary began recapping the last 48 hours as they began what would be their last drive down Elvis Presley Blvd. A few hundred mourners remained along with a ton of trash. Mary said; "if these grounds could talk oh the stories they could tell." Roger reminder her that was their job. The reporters need to convey the story these grounds would share. Roger was right, but that didn't prevent Mary from feeling a little stressed on how to pull it all together. Roger assured her she would do fine telling her to report on the funeral and the surrounding events. She should leave the speculation on the death for another time. Mary said she had no desire to stoke the fires of suspension. Reaching Forest Hills for their last view; all that remained were a few mourners and thousands of flowers lining the grounds.

Even though Lynn was no longer playing his jam box, Roger made one last request for *Fools Rush In.* Jerry quickly pointed out the song was a Ricky Nelson hit. Roger felt it was a shame because it seemed such an appropriate song considering all that had transpired. There was a change in Lynn. The jam box no longer defined him. And for Jerry, he seemed more intent on becoming an Elvis impersonator.

A small group of mourners held a sign reading *Don't forget the young girls we lost last night.* A reminder of the senseless tragedy that took place less than 24 hours earlier. Mary was encouraged someone was trying to bring attention to the girls and their deaths. There was no further discussion of the accident each processing it in their personal way, and the sadness of the occasion would stay with them for quite a while. During their short time, together all had witnessed humanity at its best and its worst.

On the way to the airport as they began to cross the Mississippi river, the silence was broken by Lynn. The Mississippi is a powerful river that flows with hopes and dreams, and it's where Lynn, decided to take a stand. Mary was frightened when Lynn called out for her to stop the car. She glanced in her mirror, but once again he said to stop the car. He said it with such conviction that Mary applied the brakes not knowing what to expect. As she began pulling over to the guard rail, Lynn's door opens, and he jumps out before the car had come to a complete stop. Once out of the car Lynn said nothing and made no eye contact he just moved toward the bridges protective railing. The scene was scary. No one knew what was going on. Lynn was making everyone nervous. Mary felt she should do something, "but what" she didn't have a clue it was all happening so fast.

Lynn was the only one who knew what was about to happen. Silence filled the air as he reached the edge of the bridge. Standing by the rail, the setting sun was bouncing off the jam box, and Lynn appeared to be studying the flowing waters for what seemed an eternity. No one said a word as Lynn acted on his plan. In a single move, he hurled the jam box and a hand full of tapes into the flowing Mississippi River. Lynn's actions surprised and shook everyone, but all were relieved it wasn't Lynn going over the rail. Lynn did not move from the railing, as he watched his prize possession begin to sink and flow with the current. It was as if time had stood still before Lynn returned to the car. No one knew what say what had come over him. All, wondered, "Why." To Mary, Lynn actions were making a statement, but what statement. Back in the car, the silence was uncomfortable. Mary felt Lynn's appearance had changed almost as if someone had lifted a large boulder from his chest. There was no doubt Lynn was pleased as he looked at everyone and smiled broadly.

Lynn pulled the door closed, and thanked Mary and told everyone that felt good. Mary glanced in the rearview mirror catching Lynn's eye as he smiled. It was then he said;

"I guessed an explanation is in order. Freedom, that's what happened freedom."

His attitude was completely different as if he had found something within himself. Lynn repeated the word freedom, freedom over and over again he was a different person and happy about it.

Jerry placed his hand on Lynn's shoulder and repeated the word freedom. Maybe Jerry knew what had taken place he, after all, was keenly aware of the relationship Lynn had with the music box. He was now free from it all it. He was free from the musical bounds of his creation free from being a fanatical fan of Elvis Presley. Lynn restated his feeling saying he was free of Elvis and the King is dead. Lynn's statement reflected his experiences in Memphis had changed him.

Mary felt everyone who came to Memphis probably changed in some way. A chapter in her life was closing, but new ones would soon begin.

As Mary pulled back into the flowing traffic, a car blew its horn bringing everyone back to the moment. Jerry says Thank you, thank you very much just as Elvis had so many times in his life. Mary couldn't help but laugh once she realized it was a Shriner that motioned them back into traffic. What a week it had been.

It was different seeing Lynn no longer connected to the large silver music box; he now looked relieved but free as well. The amateur psychologist in Mary told her Lynn had reached the point where the jam box represented a negative obsession an obsession for an entertainer whose life had many of the same problems everyone faces. His actions spoke volumes as to how he felt about the death and the funeral. Lynn told the group that no longer would he introduce himself as the head of any fan club. "I'll continue to enjoy Elvis's music, but no longer will it define my life."

Mary questioned Lynn about what it meant for him to rid himself of the box. He took a few seconds to weigh his answer, and said;

"You know when we arrived I felt Elvis was larger than life. I didn't consider him a regular person he was far more than that he was the king. But he didn't give himself that title we his adoring public did. And when you proclaim someone the king you just naturally feel they can't be affected by the normal trappings of life. In two short days, I've received an education about myself and Elvis, and there are things I learned about both of us that are not very flattering. Elvis's fame trapped him, and my hero worship trapped me. I'll never have to deal with fame and fortune, but I would never consider it a burden, hell I've even wish for it. But now I see it comes with a price. Elvis had little control of his fame, but it controlled him. Two days ago, my identity was wrapped up in an entertainer, and that's not healthy. I wanted to be here, and I wanted to say goodbye, and I did love the man and his music. But I've learned that life has a lot to offer, and we should celebrate our accomplishments show respect for others but not lose sight of our own gifts and talents. The box was a personal tribute to Elvis it was in many ways a small celebration to him and his career. But it also gave me a crutch. A crutch I used to open doors and conversations I developed an identity of being a black Elvis fan. That's not healthy, and it certainly wasn't productive".

The others were silent as Lynn continued to talk telling them;

"Elvis struggled with his demons and a demanding public. Elvis's popularity affected his life, and now his death has affected the lives of three innocent families. Those girls had their entire lives ahead of them only to be taken by some drunk fool. The hours I've spent in the heat with the other thousands of other mourners has made me realize that fame comes with a price. Elvis was no King he may have been a great singer, but he was only human."

Jerry was surprised with Lynn's talk telling him he may need to chill a little after all they had been through a lot. "Maybe I am overthinking things, but the death of the young girls bothers me, and if the rumors about Elvis's death being a hoax turn out to be true then there is no forgiving the man. When we got here, I didn't want to believe Elvis was dead, but now I don't want to believe he's alive."

Unfortunately, Mary felt Lynn was right Elvis's death might have been the result of a self-destructive lifestyle brought on by his fame.

Elvis had felt the pressure from a demanding public causing him to forget who he was.

Lynn continued;

"Hell, Elvis couldn't live a normal life even if he wanted to. He couldn't even leave his home without being mobbed. He may have had wealth and riches, but he didn't have freedom. What good is having all the money you want if you can't enjoy spending it?"

Jerry told Lynn that wasn't fair Elvis's fans loved the way he sang and entertained, but Elvis, not his public made the decisions to live life as he did. Lynn replied that might be true, but fans do influence behavior and lifestyle. He continued saying;

"Think about it Jerry we have only been out of New York a few times, and every one of them dealt with Elvis. We were fans, but we were also enablers. Even when his concerts began to suffer, we made excuses for him. We didn't want to face reality, and from what I've learned neither did he. It just seems like he was falling into a personal hell and those of us who loved him were paving the way."

Jerry said; "Damn man that's heavy." But this was how Lynn felt, and now he was feeling a sense of freedom from the chains of being a fan. He would no longer be obsessed with any entertainer. Lynn just wanted to live his life and let others live theirs.

Mary agreed with Lynn; fame does come with a price, and it seems Elvis may have paid the ultimate price. Unfortunately, having a fan base comes with demands and responsibilities. Entertainers give a lot to their fans, and in some cases, that debt comes at the cost of their freedom. Mary told Lynn; "it sounded like you are making a wise decision everyone needs to live their life, not the life of someone else."

Lynn had given an honest evaluation of the funeral and how he viewed the events. Mary began to think how she was affected by the experience. She had no idea what to expect once arriving in Memphis.

Coming to Memphis represented a major change from her normal behavior. She had always lived her life rather safely never taking many risks. But she surprised herself. She had left her comfort zone for adventure. With a ton of reasons to say no she accepted the challenge to board the plane and come to Memphis. Two days ago, she was reporting on pageants and recipes only dreaming of the big story. Then with the death of Elvis came an opportunity that she chose to accept rather giving in to fear. What led to this behavior she didn't know, but she was thankful for the experience and the lesson in life she had received. Not only did she get her story she also learned about life while covering a death. She too had been affected by the funeral and was grateful.

Mary knew her article would be secondary to the experiences she had enjoyed and the people she had met. Hopefully, the story she would write would impress her boss and in turn lead to more meaningful assignments, but the true value of her experience lived in what she had learned about life. Her time in Memphis would always be a personal highlight. What she discovered about the human spirit was far more meaningful than the work she did. She had witnessed thousands come together for a single purpose. Everyone came to Memphis with their agenda, but once arriving, they not only shared the experience but grew from it as well.

It seemed certain that everyone would be leaving with a sense of community. A community that came together to mourn the passing of Elvis Presley as well as share in the celebration of his life. Those in Memphis saw life while viewing death. Mary understood that the value of her adventure was in the friendships she had made and the emotions she had felt, not the words she would write.

HOMEWARD BOUND

ONCE THEY ARRIVED AT THE airport, it was now time to say goodbye. Mary had spent less than two full days in Memphis, but now those she met and would be saying goodbye to where friends and she felt as if she had known them her entire life.

Mary could sense Roger felt she was in deep thought. He asked; "Are you ready to write your story."

Mary acknowledges; "I've got my fears of being able to convey the true story there is so much to write about."

"Write from your heart, and you will find success."

"Well, it's been an eye-opener for sure."

Roger trying to reassure her stated; "I've covered my share of major stories, but I've got to tell you this funeral was more than an assignment it was an experience. An experience made different by the love and admiration we witnessed here in Memphis."

Roger seemed to be on the same page with Mary when he told her that she would be reporting on the death of an entertainer but felt the real story was how the entertainer affected the lives of those he left behind fans and critics. Roger believed that the final chapter in the life and career of Elvis Presley would take years to write. Those who were affected by Elvis's death would be the ones writing the chapter. To Roger, it was rather ironic that only the living can keep the memory of the dead alive. If it is true that people die twice once in the physical death and again when no one remembers them, Elvis should have a long life after death.

Roger turned his attention to Lynn telling him that his change in philosophy should serve him well. Choosing to live life not the lives of others was one of the best decisions anyone could make. Roger went on to tell Lynn;

"In life, you have a choice you can watch it go by, or you can join in. Those that join in are the true winners. Elvis may not have been able to fully experience his life, thinking of himself living under a public microscope. But in life, everyone is being watched but one's real judge is the reflection we see in the mirror, and when you look at your life pray you are satisfied with what you see."

The group came to Lynn and Jerry's gate first. Lynn's had taken on a new attitude once he trashed the jam box. Mary thought to herself his new approach looked good on him. Mary asked what the future holds for the ex-black leader of an Elvis fan club. Lynn said;

"I'm not sure, but you can bet I'm going to enjoy my new outlook. I'll always love music, but I'm going to change how I choose to honor those who create it. Now I realize that everyone has fears and problems the famous and the not so famous no one is immune to the trappings of life the good and the bad. I'm feeling good about my future. I want to thank everyone for your patience's when it came to me and my jam box."

Lynn was certainly more relaxed and less preoccupied. Lynn gave Mary a hug and thanked her for being the driver and local historian, adding she and everyone else helped make the trip memorable. Mary smiled and told Lynn his new outlook fitted him nicely.

Mary turned her attention toward Jerry and asked what his plans were. Jerry acknowledged all the talk about Elvis and his memory had gotten him to thinking. It was then he began shuffling through his bag and pulled out a white sequence jumpsuit. It was a replica of one of Elvis's fame jumpsuit worn in many concerts. Jerry smiled broadly and told them he had purchased it earlier in the day and felt it was just what he needed to jump-start a new career. The outfit was his first installment on a new singing venture. Jerry had decided to become an Elvis impersonator. Lynn couldn't hold back his laughter and asked if the suit also came with talent because he was going to need it. Mary admired the suit and told Jerry she loved it and who knows one day maybe she would see him in Vegas. They all laughed and once again shared a hug. Roger told them both it had been a real pleasure and he hoped to see them again one day. No one knew what the future held, and it mattered little on this night in Memphis two guys from New York had discovered a new slice of life.

Walking toward Mary's gate, she asked Roger what he thought of the Elvis impersonator idea. Mary questioned if there would be a market for such an act. Roger smiled and told her one thing he had learned through his years of covering the music industry there is always room for a cover band or act. Roger said maybe Jerry was just dreaming, but he would take a dream over sorrow any day. Mary loved Rogers view of life, and wondered if it was an English characteristic or just him? Roger said he wasn't sure of the answer it was a philosophy he had developed over the years. He felt life was more satisfying if you take chances and the more chances you take, the easier it becomes.

Once they reached Mary's gate, Mary knew it was going to be difficult to say goodbye. Realistically she knew they would probably never see each other again. But over the short time, they shared Mary had grown very fond of Roger and knew he could be a real friend and mentor. He was an experienced journalist who had covered major events; she could learn a so much from him. But now it was time to return to Dublin and life on the obituary desk. Before boarding the plane, Mary wondered how she could thank Roger for all he had done. She found his support, entertainment, and guidance, priceless. Roger said he should be thanking her. Mary tried to conceal her sadness by smiling. She did appreciate his insightfulness and his mannerism he was a true gentleman who also happens to be a lot of fun.

Roger took Mary's hand and told her not to underestimate her talents, he enjoyed their time together and would always be indebted to her for her knowledge of the Shriners as well as how she had stirred his interest in the hoax theories. He was glad they meet and became friends. Her talent and willingness to take a risk were two positive ingredients in life and would serve her well. Taking a risk in journalism can be good in Dublin Georgia or London England, and if she believed in herself, she would find success.

Mary knew all that was left was for her to return home and begin constructing her story for the paper. Roger assured her she did have a story to tell and felt she would do a great job. He surprised Mary when he suggested she consider doing a feature on the hoax while it was fresh in her mind he was sure there would be a market for it. He suggested she give it some attention and have some fun with it, follow up with Saunders and see if the speculation continues to grow. He added a good journalist would keep all option opened.

Still putting off getting on the plane Mary asked Roger for a favor. She wanted Roger to tell her something that may help her become a better journalist. Roger grinned and told her the question indicated she had a desire to grow. Roger said he felt she had the makeup of a good if not a great journalist. The only advice he could share with her was something he heard years ago, telling her;

"Sometimes the story comes to you, and sometimes you go to the story the important thing is no matter how you find the story always remember your audience. Treat your story as a blank canvas and know the story you paint will be viewed and shared by others be a reporter, not a participant."

Mary kissed Roger on the cheek as she hugged him. She knew she would miss him and his English accent. She suggested he come to Dublin and do a feature on small town America. He smiled and told her maybe next time. They shared laughter one last time, and before leaving he embraced her and returned her kiss taking her hand, he told her to write her story. She squeezed his hand and turned toward the gate.

Mary gave the attendant her ticket and started up the tarmac turning around once more to wave goodbye. She was welcomed by the Stewardess and began looking for her seat. She began to smile knowing that she Mary McGill did have quite a story to write. Excitement now replaced her sadness.

She was leaving Memphis with a lifetime of memories it had been a full two days. Mary knew few would believe a novice reporter from Dublin Georgia would find such adventure in Memphis Tennessee. She was lucky and thankful. All that was left was to write the story.

As Mary gazed out the window, Mary felt certain one day she would return to Memphis but knew there were few guarantees in life. It had been a wonderful adventure and a great assignment. Mary soon pulled out her souvenir T-Shirt and began to chuckle when a gentleman arrived at the seat next to her. The man took his seat and glanced at the shirt and asked if she had been in town for the funeral. Mary told him she was and then wondered if he had come to Memphis for the funeral as well. It was then he told her he had been in Memphis for a convention but could see some of the funeral adding it was quite a week. All Mary could do was agree. She then noticed the man was carrying a Shriner's hat tassels and all. Her smile quickly turns to laughter. Once she heard the stewardess began the cabin instructions, Mary closed her eyes and began to hum if *they could see me now.*

Printed in the United States
By Bookmasters